THE
SCHOOL STORY

Andrew Clements

Illustrated by Brian Selznick

ALADDIN PAPERBACKS

New York   London   Toronto   Sydney   Singapore

First Aladdin Paperbacks edition September 2002

Text copyright © 2001 by Andrew Clements
Illustrations copyright © 2001 by Brian Selznick

ALADDIN PAPERBACKS
An imprint of Simon & Schuster Children's Publishing Division
1230 Avenue of the Americas, New York, NY 10020

Also available in a Simon & Schuster Books for Young Readers hardcover edition.
Book designed by Paula Winicur
The text of this book is set in Revival.
The illustrations are rendered in pencil.

Printed in the United States of America
10 9
The Library of Congress has cataloged the hardcover edition as follows:
Clements, Andrew, 1949-
The School Story / by Andrew Clements; illustrated by Brian Selznick.
p.cm.
Summary: After twelve-year-old Natalie writes a wonderful novel,
her friend Zoe helps her devise a scheme to get it accepted at the
publishing house where Natalie's mother works as an editor.
ISBN 0-689-82594-3 (hc)
[1. Authorship—Fiction. 2. Publishers and publishing—Fiction.]
I. Selznick, Brian, ill. II. Title
PZ7.C59118 Pu 2001
[Fic]—dc 21
00-049683
ISBN 0-689-85186-3 (Aladdin pbk.)

For Stephanie Owens-Lurie and
Rick Richter—without whom, less
—A. C.

THE
SCHOOL STORY

CHAPTER 1

Fan Number One

Natalie couldn't take it. She peeked in the doorway of the school library, then turned, took six steps down the hall, turned, paced back, and stopped to look in at Zoe again. The suspense was torture.

Zoe was still reading. The first two chapters only added up to twelve pages. Natalie leaned against the door frame and chewed on her thumbnail. She thought, *What's taking her so long?*

Zoe could see Natalie out of the corner of her eye. She could feel all that nervous energy nudging at her, but Zoe wasn't about to be rushed. She always read slowly, and she liked it that way, especially when it was a good story. And this one was good.

The Cheater by Natalie Nelson
page 12

I catch up with Sean between Eighty-second and Eighty-first Streets. His legs are longer than mine, so I'm panting. I grab his arm and he stops in front of a bodega.

He says, "Why are you following me?"

"I've got to talk to you."

"Yeah, well, too bad. You had your chance to talk during the Penalty Board hearing. And you didn't."

"But if I told the truth, then the whole school would know I cheated. I'd get expelled."

He just looks at me. "But you really did cheat, right? . . . And I really didn't steal that answer key, right? . . . And you know I didn't steal it because *you* did, right?"

I nod yes to all the questions.

Sean is almost shouting now, his eyes wild. "So first you steal, then you cheat, and now you've lied. And me? You've left me to take the punishment."

The shopkeeper is worried. He moves from the counter to the doorway of the bodega, looking at us.

Sean ignores him and gets right into my face, screaming. "Well, guess what, Angela. We're not friends now—and I don't know if we ever were!"

He storms away, hands jammed in his pockets, shoulders hunched, stabbing the sidewalk with every step.

Me, I cry.

Zoe let page twelve slip onto the table and then stared at it, deep in thought.

"So, what do you think?"

Natalie was right behind her, and Zoe jumped six inches. "Jeez, Natalie! Scare me to death! And you ruined a nice moment too."

"But what do you think? Is it any good?"

Zoe nodded. "I think it's very good."

"Really?" Natalie pulled out a chair and sat down, leaning forward. "I mean, you're not just saying that because we're best friends?"

Zoe shook her head. "No, I mean it. It's good. Like I can't wait to read the whole thing. Can you bring the rest tomorrow?"

Natalie smiled and reached into her backpack. She pulled out a blue folder with a rubber band around it. "Here. I've still got to write about five more chapters. I just needed to know if the beginning was any good, but you can read what I've got done if you want."

Zoe took the folder carefully and said, "This is great. But you *are* going to finish it, right? Do you know the whole story already—like all the way to the end?"

Natalie said, "Not *all* the way to the end . . . but almost. I know how the end *feels*, but not exactly what happens—at least, not yet."

Natalie's book had begun by accident on the bus with her mom late one afternoon back in

September. Sixth grade was already three weeks old, and both she and her mom had settled into the routine of commuting together. It was a Friday afternoon, and they were going home on the 5:55 coach, thundering through the Lincoln Tunnel from New York City to Hoboken, New Jersey.

Her mom looked exhausted. Natalie studied the face tilted toward her on the headrest. It was a pretty face—*Prettier than mine*, she thought. But there were little lines at the corners of her mother's eyes and mouth. Care lines, worry lines.

Natalie said, "Hard day, Mom?"

Eyes still closed, her mom smiled and nodded. "The editorial department met all day with the marketing department—all day."

Natalie asked, "How come?" When her dad died, Natalie had decided she needed to talk to her mom more. Sometimes she pretended to be interested in her mom's work at the publishing company even when she wasn't. Like now.

Her mom said, "Well, the marketing people keep track of what kinds of books kids and parents and teachers are buying. Then they tell us, and we're supposed to make more books like the ones they think people will buy."

Natalie said, "Makes sense. So, what kinds of books do they want you to make?"

Hannah Nelson lifted her head off the seat back and turned toward Natalie. "Here's the summary of a six-hour meeting. Ready?"

Natalie nodded.

Her mom used a deep voice that sounded bossy. "People, we need to publish more adventure books, more series books, and more school stories." In her regular voice she said, "That was it. A six-hour meeting for something that could have gone into a one-page memo—or a three-line E-mail."

Then Natalie asked, "What's a school story?"

"A school story is just what it sounds like—it's a short novel about kids and stuff that happens mostly at school."

Natalie thought for a second and then said, "You mean like *Dear Mr. Henshaw*?"

And her mom said, "Exactly."

Then Natalie said to herself, *Hey, who knows more about school than someone who's right there, five days a week, nine months a year? I bet I could write a school story.*

And that was all it took. Natalie Nelson the novelist was born.

Or almost born. Her career as an author didn't officially spring to life until about four months later—on that afternoon in the school library after Zoe read the first two chapters.

Because it's the same for every new author, for every new book. Somebody has to be the first to read it. Somebody has to be the first to say she likes it. Somebody has to be that first fan.

And of course, that was Zoe.

CHAPTER 2

A Portrait of the Author as a Young Girl

Some
people are writers, and some people
are talkers. Natalie had always been a writer.

Like all writers, first she was a reader. As a baby
and then a toddler, Natalie loved it when her mom

or dad read to her. She loved how the same story would change, depending on who was reading it.

Mom read calmly, evenly, thoughtfully. Even if the story was exciting or scary or sad, Natalie always felt warm and safe when Mom was reading.

But not with Dad. He was loud and reckless. He made funny voices for all the firemen and ducks and princesses. He made sound effects for the trains and the caterpillars, and if the words weren't exciting or silly or scary enough, he threw in some new ones. When Dad was reading, anything could happen.

And so Natalie got her first taste of reading in the very best way, from people who loved good books almost as much as they loved her.

By the time she was four, Natalie couldn't wait any longer. She wanted more stories than her parents had time to read to her. She already knew her ABCs, and she made her mom and dad point at every word as they read to her. Then Natalie would sit and turn the pages of her picture books again and again. She started being able to see the words and hear the sounds they made, and once she began to crack the code, there was no stopping her. Natalie became a reader.

Even after Natalie could read by herself, her mom and dad read stories to her at bedtime—Dad one night, and Mom the next. Natalie always got to choose the story from her shelf of favorites.

The car crash changed all that. Natalie was in second grade, and after the accident there was only Mom to read at bedtime. And that was when Natalie hid some of her favorite books in the back of her closet. She didn't want her mom to read them anymore. Those were Daddy's books. Sometimes late at night, or on a quiet Sunday afternoon, Natalie would open up *The Sailor Dog* or *The Grouchy Ladybug*, and she could hear her father's voice reading to her.

The writing part came gradually, naturally. At first it was imitation. If Natalie read a good poem, she tried to make up one like it. If a character grabbed her imagination, Natalie would talk to her stuffed animals and pretend she was the Sailor Dog or the Steadfast Tin Soldier or Raggedy Ann. She would act out parts of a story and make up words for everyone to say. Sometimes she pretended to be Gretel, helping Hansel push the wicked witch into the oven. Other times she pretended to be the wicked witch.

And always, always, Natalie thought about the authors. She thought about Hans Christian Andersen or Margaret Wise Brown or Beatrix Potter, and she imagined these people sitting in a garden or a cabin or an attic, making up new stories. And she knew that one day she would sit down in a garden or a cabin or an attic and try it out for herself.

When Natalie got to fourth grade, she began to spend more time writing. She made herself a little writing place in the back corner of the loft that she and her mom had moved to. Her desk was a door laid flat across two small filing cabinets. She sat in her dad's old red desk chair and used his old Macintosh computer. Not quite a cabin or an attic, but close enough—and it was as close as Natalie could get to her dad.

CHAPTER 3

Mystery Man

"So, what are you going to do with the book," asked Zoe, "you know, when it's all finished?"

"Don't know yet." Natalie gathered up the first twelve pages from the library table in front of Zoe. "Maybe print out a copy for you, and maybe one for Lill and Sparky . . . maybe let some other kids read it. I might even show it to Ms. Clayton—maybe get some extra credit in English." Natalie handed the pages to Zoe, and she tucked them into the blue folder with the rest of the manuscript.

Zoe shook her head, and her curly brown hair bounced from side to side. "It's way too good for that. I think you should get it all done and then give it to your mom. She should get it published—you know, for real."

Natalie snorted. "Yeah, like my mom is going to take it to her boss and say, 'Guess what? My daughter wrote this wonderful little book,' and then her boss goes, 'Gee, that's great—let's pay her a bunch of money and start printing her book right away!' Get real, Zoe. You don't know anything about publishing."

"Do too," said Zoe. "My dad gets this magazine called *Publishers Weekly* at his office, and when I go there, I read all about what the bestsellers are and who's making the big deals." Zoe's dad was a lawyer, and she always bragged to Natalie about big deals and famous clients.

Natalie shook her head. "Well, I've seen that magazine too, *and* I've also been to my mom's office at her publishing company, and I've seen stacks and stacks of envelopes filled with new books from new authors, and most of them don't get published. So there!"

"Shhh!" Mr. Levy glared at the girls from his perch at the front desk. Even though it was after three on a Thursday afternoon and they were the only kids in the room, it was still his library, and he liked it quiet.

Natalie whispered, "Let's go."

Zoe never admitted that there was something she did not know or could not do. They gathered up their coats and backpacks, and by the time they had walked halfway down the stairs toward the front door of the school, Zoe had a good idea—no, a *great* idea. But she wasn't going to just blurt it out. What's the fun of that? Zoe wanted to make Natalie work for it.

So she said, "I know how to get your book published."

Natalie shifted her backpack to the other shoulder and glanced sideways at Zoe. She said, "Oh, really?" There was just a trace of sarcasm, but Zoe heard it loud and clear.

Zoe said, "Yes, really."

Natalie and Zoe had been best friends since their first day of kindergarten at the Deary School. From the start it had been a push-and-pull friendship, the kind that can happen when two very different people like each other a lot.

They stepped out onto the sidewalk. It was sunny, but a cold wind whipped across the

Hudson River and skittered off the buildings on Riverside Drive. January in New York wasn't picnic weather. Pulling up the hood of her parka, Natalie said, "So, what's your big idea?"

Zoe said, "Ever hear of Ted Geisel?"

Natalie shook her head and said, "No . . . does he go to school here?"

Zoe looked amazed, shocked. She put her hands on her hips and said, "You mean you've never heard of Ted Geisel? Really? Well. Then *that's* your homework assignment."

Natalie laughed. "You don't have an idea at all—you're just trying to send me on some wild goose chase."

Zoe shook her head and put on an air of superiority. "No, I really *do* have a plan, and it's a very good plan. But until you know who Ted Geisel is, it won't make any sense to you. So go learn what you have to learn, and we'll talk about it tomorrow, maybe."

Natalie lifted her nose into the air and said, "Fine!" She turned on her heel and headed south. She had to walk down to Seventy-second Street and then east to Broadway to catch a bus to her mom's office in midtown. Most of the schoolkids in the city used the subway. It was a lot faster, but Natalie always felt too closed in down there. Besides, the buses smelled better. Natalie was never in a rush anyway. Today, like almost every school day, it would be about another three hours before she got home.

Zoe would be home in twenty minutes, and all she had to do was put up her hand. When she did, a yellow cab pulled out of the traffic on Riverside Drive. It veered over and lurched to a stop at the curb. Zoe lived on East Sixty-fifth Street, and she always went home in a taxi. As Zoe opened the rear door of the cab she yelled to Natalie, "Remember—Ted Geisel!"

Natalie was almost to the first cross street. She looked back over her shoulder, made a face, and stuck out her tongue. Then she turned and kept walking, smiling to herself.

Zoe could be a pain, but once in a while she really did come up with a great idea. Natalie couldn't wait to find out something about this Ted Geisel.

CHAPTER 4

City Kid

Natalie's mom was nervous when her twelve-year-old daughter had to get around New York City on her own—so she was nervous almost every afternoon. She didn't like it, but she didn't have any choice. Every weekday morning she put Natalie into a taxi at the bus station. The cab drove straight uptown to the Deary School at a time of day when most of the traffic was going the other direction. Even so, that ride still cost about nine dollars. But an afternoon cab ride to her office building near Rockefeller Center took much longer, and the fare was almost twice as much. Hannah Nelson just couldn't afford to pay that much for transportation every single school day.

She worried, but she knew Natalie was a good city kid—always had been. Back when Natalie was only three and they still lived in Manhattan, her dad had taught her to look for a police officer if she ever got lost. If she couldn't see a police officer, Natalie learned she should talk only to a lady with children, because a mother or a nanny would always help a lost child. She also learned how to dial collect from a pay phone and how to use 911. Her dad had taught her well.

Natalie knew she had to be careful in the city, but she also knew that she didn't have to walk around feeling afraid all the time. She felt fine about her daily trip to her mom's office. She was tall for a girl of twelve and looked as if she might be fourteen or fifteen. She had plenty of street smarts, but she was also well equipped. Natalie had a whistle on the lanyard around her neck and a twenty-dollar bill under the liner in her left shoe. Hannah Nelson also made her daughter carry an emergency cell phone. Natalie could push one button that sent a message to the police, to her mom at the office, and to her uncle Fred. Fred Nelson was her dad's younger brother, and he'd made a point of spending time with Natalie ever since the accident. He lived a few blocks from the Deary School, and his office was on Madison Avenue. If there was ever a problem, Natalie would have plenty of help.

Still, at least once a week her mom would remind Natalie of the basic rules: If a person begins bothering you, yell and start running. Never get into a car or a van, and if someone asks you to come closer, run the other way. Always stay on the main streets, where there are plenty of people. If someone ever grabs hold of you, bite, scratch, kick, scream—do whatever it takes to get away, and then run, keep calling for help, and hit 911 on the cell phone. Don't get into an empty bus or an overcrowded one. Sit or stand at the front, near the driver. Never go into a strange building.

Like most city kids, Natalie had developed a kind of radar. Scanning the sidewalk ahead of her, if she saw a person who looked shady or someone asking for money or acting pushy or weird, she'd find a way to avoid a face-to-face meeting. If she had to, she could always cross the street, but usually it was just a matter of watching for the right moment to pass by. At age twelve, and after years of walking in New York, avoiding trouble had become almost automatic for Natalie.

Still, it's impossible to plan for everything. There was the time a woman on the bus started yelling at Natalie's backpack like it was a dog that was trying to bite her. Natalie was scared, but she stayed calm. When the driver shouted, "Hey, lady—shut up or get off!" the lady got off and started screaming at a trash can on the corner. And then there was the time Natalie thought this tall boy wearing sunglasses was following her. He walked behind her all the way from Seventy-ninth Street to the bus stop at Seventy-second Street and Broadway. When he took the same bus she did, Natalie got really scared. She thought he was looking at her from behind his dark glasses. Just when she was about to ask the bus driver for help, the boy stood up and got off at the next stop, and Natalie saw him walk into a big bookstore on Fifty-seventh Street. False alarm.

Today's trip was uneventful, and when Natalie got to the lobby of her mom's building, she signed in at the desk, got in the elevator, and pushed the button for the fourteenth floor. The elevator hummed up to the third floor, and three more people got on. They pushed the buttons for floors five, seven, and eight. People got on and off the elevator at almost every floor, and soon Natalie was squeezed against the back wall.

The first time she had come to visit her mom at work was about four years earlier. Back then Natalie was sure that making children's books had to be the most exciting job in the world. Natalie had expected to see mountains of books and a huge, noisy workshop. Some people would be painting book covers, others would be printing and folding the pages, and over in a corner someone would be gluing everything together.

What she actually saw on that first visit was a large, quiet room filled with a maze of little offices. Here and there small groups talked quietly at large tables, and everywhere people sat at computer screens, tapping away. True, there were plenty of books around—stacks and boxes and bookcases of them—but they were all finished. Natalie was disappointed. A publishing company was a pretty boring place.

The elevator door opened on fourteen, and Natalie stepped out onto the thick green carpet of the reception area. The receptionist was talking into his headset, but he gave her a smile and a wave, and then pushed the security button. The door to the right began to buzz. Natalie pushed it open and walked into the editorial department of Shipley Junior Books.

The sign beside the opening of her mom's small, windowless office said HANNAH NELSON, EDITOR. The room had a door and a ceiling, but in all other respects it was a basic cubicle. The office contained a desktop that made a U, and bookcases lined the walls. Every inch of space was loaded with piles of paper and books. There was a

computer, two small filing cabinets, one swivel chair, a plastic trash basket, and one straight-backed chair just inside the doorway. All the furniture was gray or green.

Balanced above the computer screen was a single photograph in a clear plastic holder—Dad and Mom and Natalie in a sailboat. Every time she came to the office, that picture was the first thing Natalie saw. All three of them looked like they were having such a good time, but Natalie couldn't remember being there. She always wished she could.

"Hi, Mom."

Hannah Nelson spun around in her chair and pulled Natalie into a hug. She held both of her daughter's hands a moment and then reached up to push a wisp of brownish blond hair out of Natalie's eyes. "Have you had a good day, sweetheart?"

Natalie nodded. "Except everyone gave a ton of homework. Can I go get a snack?"

"Uh-huh . . . here." Her mom swung her chair around, pulled open a drawer, and swiveled back. She handed Natalie a small stack of quarters. "Could you get me a Sprite, or maybe some apple juice? You can start your homework in Ella's office. She's away all week."

It was fifteen minutes later—soda drained and cookies gone—before Natalie remembered Zoe's assignment. She jumped up out of Ella's chair, grabbed a dictionary from the shelf near the doorway, and flipped to the Gs. *Game, gargoyle, geisha*—no *Geisel.*

Turning around, Natalie sat down at the desk and moved the mouse next to the keyboard, and the darkened computer screen jumped to life. She'd used Ella's computer before, so she knew what to look for. She clicked on a folder labeled REFERENCE and then clicked again on ENCARTA.

The encyclopedia opened up, and a few clicks later she had it in search mode. Natalie typed *Geisel,* and then hit the return key.

And there he was: *Geisel, Theodor.* End of mystery.

CHAPTER 5

The Plot Thickens

"Dr. Seuss."

Those were Natalie's first words to Zoe on Friday, whispered during the morning meeting.

When Natalie had discovered that Theodor Geisel was the real name of Dr. Seuss, at first she didn't see Zoe's point. She thought about it on the bus ride home Thursday, and then off and on all night. By Friday morning Natalie had a pretty good idea why Zoe had made her learn about Ted Geisel.

But as the morning meeting ended and they headed toward the science rooms, Natalie pretended she didn't have a clue. That way, Zoe could explain everything. Natalie knew that was what Zoe always preferred.

"So, do you get it?" asked Zoe.

Natalie looked at her blankly. "Get what?"

"The idea—you know—Ted Geisel, Dr. Seuss?" prompted Zoe. "You can get your book published by using a different name. That way your mom won't know it's you! She reads, she likes, she publishes! Great idea, right? You get to pick a pseudonym, a phony name!"

Natalie paused a few seconds, then said, "You mean I get to lie to my mom, right?"

Zoe made a face. "Oh, come on."

Zoe and Natalie had different ideas about what was and was not a lie. Natalie always got the best results with the whole truth. Zoe wasn't a liar, but as long as the truth was not entirely absent, Zoe felt just fine. They'd had this discussion before, and Natalie usually held out for complete honesty.

But today Zoe was prepared. She said, "Okay, tell me this: Was Dr. Seuss lying to forty gazillion kids just because they didn't know his real name? Was that a lie?"

Natalie started to reply, but Zoe kept on building her case. "Was Samuel Clemens lying when everybody thought some guy named Mark Twain wrote *Huckleberry Finn*? It's not lying, Natalie. Authors use made-up names all the time. And you're an author, so it's okay."

Natalie said, "Well . . . but do you think Ted Geisel lied to his *mother*? Don't you think *she* knew he was also Dr. Seuss?"

Zoe had to think about that, but only for a few seconds. She said, "Yeah, but . . . but I bet his mother wasn't an editor. If she was, and if he sent her a bunch of his wacky pictures and stories, she'd probably have said, 'Oh, Ted—this is cute, but it's not really a book. Now, you run along outside and play baseball.' And then millions of kids would never have gotten to read *The Cat in the Hat* or *Green Eggs and Ham* or anything. All because he forgot to use a pseudonym. I bet if his mom had been an editor, he'd have kept his real name a secret—at least for a while. Remember, Natalie, she's not just your mom. She's your *editor*."

Zoe reached behind her chair and pulled the blue folder out of her backpack. She handed it to Natalie and said, "Here. I stayed up until eleven last night to read it. It's great, even better than I thought it would be. And I can't wait until it's finished. It's going to make a great book."

Natalie was quiet as she sat down at their worktable in science class. Zoe could feel victory, but she didn't want to rush things. Zoe knew better. Natalie always had to think things through for herself. So Zoe pretended to be busy with her lab notebook and then started assembling the string and weights they would need for their experiment about simple machines.

Natalie put the manuscript away. As she slowly pulled her science book from her backpack she said, "Cassandra . . . Cassandra Day. I've always wished my name could be Cassandra. Do you think Cassandra Day is a good name?"

Zoe grinned. "It's a *great* name!" She stuck out her hand, and when Natalie took it, Zoe pumped it up and down and said, "Cassandra Day, I'm so glad to get to meet such a wonderful author!"

CHAPTER 6

Reality Attack

Zoe's excitement was like a river. All day Friday it swept Natalie along. But after school, alone, riding the bus to her mom's office, Natalie started to face facts.

First of all, her book wasn't finished. And even when it was, would it be something a real editor would want to look at? Just because Zoe liked it, that didn't mean her mom would. And what if other people thought the book was really bad?

By the time Natalie arrived at Shipley Junior Books, she had talked herself out of the whole crazy idea. Standing in the opening of Ella's cubicle, Natalie sipped on a strawberry-kiwi drink and looked at the mounds of mail from writers all over the country. Brown envelopes, white envelopes, red-and-gold envelopes with fancy lettering. Manuscripts from writers in California and Illinois and Texas and Florida. Hundreds of them. Some of them had been mailed more than six months ago. Some of the envelopes hadn't even been opened. It was like a morgue for dead books.

Natalie finished her drink and slumped down into Ella's chair. She picked up the phone, punched "9," then dialed Zoe's number, the one for her private line in her bedroom. Zoe actually had two private phone numbers, because she also had her own cell phone. Zoe picked up during the first ring.

"Zoe Reisman's room at the Reisman residence, Zoe Reisman speaking."

"Zoe? It's me. It's a stupid idea."

"What?"

"Trying to get my story published—it's a stupid idea, Zoe. Even if I get the book done, and even if it's halfway decent, no one will ever read it, and even if they read it, there are probably a million books that are better. So what's the point?"

It was silent on the other end of the line.

Natalie said, "Zoe? Are you there?"

Zoe's voice was hard. "Let me talk to Cassandra Day."

"Give it up, Zoe. Cassandra Day is dead."

Zoe was fierce now. "If you don't put Cassandra Day on the phone this instant, then I'm going to call the police and tell them that a girl who looks

just like you is hiding there in that building on the fourteenth floor and has kidnapped an amazingly talented person named Cassandra Day. Now you just put Cassandra on the line, or the next thing you'll hear is sirens."

Natalie smiled. She knew Zoe wasn't going to let up, so she paused a moment. Then in a quiet voice a little deeper than her own she said, "Yes? This is Cassandra Day."

Zoe said, "Thank God you're all right! Now listen, Cassie—"

Natalie broke in, enjoying her new voice. "Oh, my . . . no, no, no, dear. No one *ever* calls me *Cassie*. It's Cassandra, always Cassandra."

Zoe never liked being interrupted, but she held on to her focus. "Fine. Okay, Cassandra. Listen, Cassandra. Don't you believe one thing

that that deadbeat Natalie tells you. You are a great writer. One day your grandchildren are going to read all the books you've written. And we are going to get this first one published, okay? You've got to trust me on this. Are you with me?"

Natalie sighed, but still speaking as Cassandra she said, "Yes, I am with you. . . . But I must say that you are an extremely annoying and cantankerous person."

"Miss Day, let me worry about me. You just make sure you keep your head clear. Now, you go home and do some writing this weekend, okay?"

Natalie didn't answer. Five seconds. Ten seconds.

Zoe said, "Cassandra? . . . You *are* going to go home and finish another chapter this weekend—right?"

"I guess so. Sure. I'll keep writing."

"And Cassandra?"

"What?" said Natalie.

"I'm proud to know you, Cassandra. Goodbye."

"Thanks, Zoe. Bye."

CHAPTER 7

Business Lesson

Cassandra Day was still alive, but she wasn't exactly in tip-top shape. After saying good-bye to Zoe, Natalie sat in Ella's chair, staring at the stacks of unread manuscripts, imagining what it would be like to have her own story there among them. It was too depressing, so she went to her mom's office and sat on the chair just inside the doorway. Her mom was absorbed in a manuscript, leaning over the stack of paper, red pencil in one hand, gum eraser in the other. Natalie didn't want to interrupt her, but she had to. She cleared her throat and said, "Mom, what's with that big stack of envelopes? Are they all manuscripts?"

Hannah looked up from her work and said, "The ones in Ella's office, or the ones over in Tim's space?"

Natalie's mouth dropped open. "You mean there are more?"

Her mom smiled. "Lots more. You put them all together and it's called the slush pile. When someone sends us something without asking us first if we want to see it, it goes into the slush pile. Those are called unsolicited submissions. Someone writes a story, thinks it should be published, sticks it in an envelope, finds our address in a reference book or somewhere, and sends it off to New York City. The people in the mail room bring us nine or ten new ones every single day, and twice as many on Mondays."

Natalie asked, "Does anyone ever read them?"

Her mom nodded. "Eventually. Everyone will at least get a letter that says thanks, but no thanks. Digging through the slush pile is one of the jobs you get when you're brand-new in the editorial department. Whenever Ella and Tim have some time, they chip away at it. When it gets too huge, we get a couple of interns from NYU or Brooklyn College and have them power through the whole stack. Most of those people get sent a rejection letter."

Natalie frowned. "It doesn't seem fair. How can someone just take a quick look and right away say no?"

Her mom was about to answer, when Letha appeared in the doorway. Ignoring Natalie, she said, "Hannah, I need that Trevor manuscript on my desk before you leave today. Are you nearly done?" Letha Springfield was Hannah's boss, the editor in chief at Shipley Junior Books. She stood there, one eyebrow arched, arms folded. Natalie's eyes were drawn to Letha's long fingernails, bloodred against the pale yellow silk of her blouse.

Hannah said, "I'll be done with it in about an hour . . . will that be all right?"

Letha smiled, but there was no warmth. She said, "I really needed it yesterday. . . ." Then glancing at Natalie, she continued, "But I know you're very busy. Just be sure I have it today, all right?" And then she was gone. Natalie stared at the dents that the woman's high heels had left in the carpet.

Hannah said, "Gotta get back to work, sweetheart. Try to stay out of sight, okay?"

• • • • •

Settled next to her mom on the bus an hour and a half later, Natalie said, "I still want to know how a person in your office can take one quick look at someone's story and decide it's a reject. That's not fair."

"I used to think that too," said her mom, "but then I spent a week or so working on the slush pile myself. With ninety-nine percent of them you can tell it's not good enough after reading one page, or even less. Bad writing, weak characters, old idea, dull plot. It's pretty discouraging. Then once in a great while you open up an envelope and you find a story that has some originality, some real style. The good ones stand out like roses in a snowbank. And if you find only one like that, then you know why we keep reading the slush pile."

Natalie shook her head. "But if so few of them are any good, where do you get all the books you publish every year?"

"Well, first of all, there are writers we know, good ones we've worked with. Or authors who have written for other publishers. When an established writer sends us something, it doesn't go into the slush pile. We look at it right away.

We don't always publish it, because it still has to be right for us. But it always gets looked at seriously. And then there are new stories that agents send us."

"Agents?" asked Natalie. "Like FBI agents?"

Her mom laughed. "No, like literary agents. Agents work for writers—illustrators, too. An agent brings us something he or she thinks is good, and if we buy it, then the writer or the artist pays the agent part of the money. Most of the new books we publish come from agents."

Natalie nodded and turned to look out the window of the bus. There wasn't much to see. They were crawling along in heavy traffic, midway through the Lincoln Tunnel. The orange glow of the tunnel lights bounced off the tiles on the ceiling and walls. Natalie always imagined the boats and barges steaming along on the Hudson River above them, and she thought about the enormous weight of all that water pressing down on the tunnel. It made her feel trapped.

So did the business lesson from her mom. It was more fun back when she didn't know anything, back when a bookstore was like a wonderland and new books just kept showing up like magic.

At home that night, when dinner and dishes were done, Natalie went to the video store with her mom and they rented two movies. Natalie Nelson didn't feel like writing at all, and by Saturday morning Cassandra Day was nowhere to be found.

CHAPTER 8

A Portrait of the Bulldog as a Young Girl

Some people are talkers, and some people are writers. Zoe had always been a talker.

Like all talkers, first she was a listener. She listened to her mom. She listened to her two sisters. She listened to her nanny. She listened to her dad. And even before she knew any real

Deary School

IDENTIFICATION

Reisman
Zoe

GRADE SIX

words, she joined every conversation, waving her hands and gurgling.

Zoe's first word was "da"—and everyone assumed it meant "Dad." But really it was an all-purpose word. For a while everything was "da." Or "Da-da?" Or "Da! Da-da-da!" As Zoe's vocabulary grew she learned that talking had a purpose. It was how to give orders, how to let people know what she wanted. Zoe's first sentence was "Have dat!" And by the time Zoe was three, her two older sisters knew better than to get in an argument with her. Zoe always won. Always.

Like Natalie, Zoe loved books too. Her mom and her nanny read to her all the time when she was little. But Zoe never tried to imagine herself as an author. She had no interest in that. Instead she imagined what it would be like to talk to the authors. She wished she could pick up the phone and ask Roald Dahl how come James didn't find a giant pickle instead of a giant peach. *James and the Giant Pickle.* Now *that* would have been a *really* funny book.

When Zoe's parents went to their first conference with her preschool teacher, there wasn't much good news. Zoe was not very good at sharing. Zoe had trouble listening to others. Zoe would not put her hand up and wait to be called on. She just talked. When the teacher began to read a book to the class, if Zoe had already heard it, she would say, "I know this story," and then blurt out how it ended.

And Zoe always argued. She argued about the snacks. She argued about nap time. She argued about which puppet was the best puppet. Endlessly arguing. The teacher said, "For example, she's learned the names of the primary colors all right, but she argues with us about the names of the secondary colors. Zoe insists that purple should be called grapy, and orange should be called juicy. We're just trying to get her ready for school, you know, and I have to say that the staff and I have some concerns."

In the cab going home Zoe's mom was concerned too. Amy Reisman shook her head. "I knew it. We've been spoiling her. I should have spent more time with Zoe. I should have taught her how to get along better."

But Zoe's dad said, "Relax. There's nothing wrong with Zoe. She's plenty smart, and once she figures out that she needs to work with other people in this world, she'll do fine."

It turned out that both her parents were right. Zoe was a little spoiled and a little headstrong, but when she met Natalie Nelson in kindergarten, she learned very quickly that if she wanted to have a friend, she couldn't have her own way all of the time—just *most* of the time.

On Saturday morning Zoe woke up at seven. First she remembered it was Saturday. She turned over and started to go back to sleep. Then she remembered about Natalie's book. Zoe sat straight up, instantly awake. Cassandra Day was still in danger, so it would have to be Zoe to the rescue.

Zoe got up, got dressed, and then did a quick cleanup of about half the mess in her room, just in case her mom decided to make an inspection tour. She was pretty sure her dad would be going to his office, and she wanted to go with him. Her dad worked late almost every night, and Sunday was usually spent with the whole family. Zoe adored her dad, and if she wanted to get some time alone with him, it had to be on Saturday. And besides, today she really needed to go to his office.

Zoe's bedroom was the smallest one on the third floor of her family's brownstone. She closed her door silently, tiptoed past her sisters' rooms, and headed down the stairs. At the second-floor landing she smelled coffee.

When Zoe opened the first-floor door to the kitchen, her dad looked up from his newspaper, mug in one hand, and smiled at her. "Hello there, Miss Early Bird. Are you my assistant this morning?"

Zoe beamed at him and said, "I thought I was your partner, not just your assistant."

"Oops—my mistake." He gave Zoe a one-armed hug and a coffee-flavored kiss on the cheek. "You hurry up and grab some breakfast, partner. Then we'll leave a note for your mom and hit the street."

It was about eight o'clock when Zoe and her dad left the house, so the city was still pretty quiet. They walked west to Lexington Avenue, hailed a cab, and rode down to Forty-sixth and Third. Zoe didn't talk much on the cab ride or on the elevator ride up to the forty-seventh floor. She was too busy thinking, and her dad seemed to know it. Most of the time Zoe thought her dad was easy to be with. If she felt like talking, so did he. If she was quiet, he was too. That's what made it easy.

Robert Reisman was the senior managing partner at his law firm. The offices of Crouch, Pruitt, and Reisman were modest but well appointed. To Zoe, the place seemed huge. There was a comfortable reception area with a leather couch and a pair of deep armchairs. There was a library with tall bookcases and a ladder that rolled along on a track. There was a big conference room with a long wooden table. There were smaller conference rooms and lots of offices for the associates and junior members, and there was even a spiral staircase that went from the forty-seventh floor down to the rest of the offices and the filing area on the forty-sixth.

Zoe thought her dad's office was the best. From his windows she could look down the East River all the way to the Brooklyn Bridge. Sometimes Zoe would sit on the broad windowsill for an hour watching the boats and the helicopters and listening to her dad talk on the phone. He was a talker too, and like Zoe, he was good at winning arguments.

Today her dad had a lot of E-mail to answer, so Zoe made herself scarce. She went to the reception area and poked through the magazines until she found what she was looking for: a recent issue of *Publishers Weekly*. She hadn't been lying when she told Natalie that she'd read the magazine at her dad's office. But she hadn't ever looked at it carefully. She took the issue into the main conference room, closed both doors, and sat in the big armchair at the head of the table. Spreading the magazine out before her, she turned past sixteen pages of ads before she found the table of contents.

Flipping from section to section, Zoe read part of an article about horror books. Then she read about a deal to make a movie out of a children's book. There were pages and pages of ads everywhere and a whole lot of reviews of new books—fiction books, nonfiction books, travel books, mystery books, children's books, history books, and on and on and on.

After almost an hour of reading, Zoe felt like her head was spinning. Looking in the magazine reminded her of when she had looked under a big, flat rock at their farm in Connecticut last summer. She had seen thousands of little ants and bugs running every which way. There were paths and tunnels, tiny rooms and bigger rooms, with workers scurrying all over the place carrying twigs and leaves and eggs—a whole little world. And now she was peeking into the world of books and the people who make them. Zoe had to admit it. Publishing wasn't so simple after all.

Zoe had won the argument with Natalie about trying to get her book published, and then she had won the argument about not giving up. Shaking her head, Zoe thought, *But what now? Natalie's book is really good, and I want to help her, but how?*

Zoe walked out of the conference room, put the magazine back, and went into her dad's office. He was looking at the notebook computer on his desk, tapping away, his reading glasses perched on the end of his nose. Zoe flopped down on the sofa beside the tall windows.

When her father paused and looked up at

her, Zoe said, "Dad, if you wrote a book, how would you get it published?"

He looked at her. "Me? A book? Why would I want to write a book? I'm never going to write a book."

"Okay, okay, but let's say that you *did* write a book. How would you get it published?"

Her dad pushed back from his desk and slowly swiveled his chair back and forth. He narrowed his eyes and scratched his chin. Zoe loved watching her dad think. He pursed his lips and said, "What kind of a book?"

Zoe shrugged. "How should I know—any kind of a book."

Her dad smiled. "All right, then. First of all, what do I always tell you? I tell you that up to a certain point, it's not *what* you know, but *who* you know. So first I'd get a great agent, a real bulldog. The kind of agent who won't take no for an answer. Then we'd map out a strategy, we'd target the best people at the best publishers. Then I just point my bulldog at the red meat, and I say, 'Go get 'em!' That's the 'who you know' part. That's why you hire an agent. It's the agent's job to get the book to the right person so the book gets a fair shot. After that the book has to stand on its own, right?"

Zoe nodded and said, "Right."

"So if the book's any good, and it gets into the right hands, then *Boom!*—it gets published. Any questions?"

Zoe shook her head.

Then her dad said, "So what got you going on this?"

"Oh . . . just curious. I found a copy of *Publishers Weekly* out in the reception room, and it got me thinking." Zoe knew this wasn't the whole truth, but it was enough for now.

Her dad scooched his chair back toward his desk. "Well, I'll be done here in another five minutes or so. You ready to go?"

Zoe nodded. "Whenever you are."

Zoe was quiet on the cab ride home. She was busy thinking, and for Zoe, that meant she was arguing with herself: *First of all, Natalie's book is good. How come you're so sure about that? Because I am. Can you think of any books you've read that are better? No? So, like I said, the book is good. So that means if the book gets to the right editor, the editor will like it, right? Right. So all we have to do is find an agent to make sure that Cassandra Day's first novel gets looked at, right? Right.*

The rest of the weekend Zoe was busy. She spent some time searching for information on the Internet, and she spent some time using the computer and the printer in her mom and dad's little office in the study on the second floor of her house. And she spent a lot of time thinking.

Zoe wanted to get this book published. Sure, she loved the challenge of it. But there was more. She didn't want to do it just to prove she could get it done. It was something she wanted to do for Natalie, something for Natalie and her mom.

Because Zoe saw things. When you stay friends for a long time, you see things. Zoe remembered Natalie's dad. He was not someone you could forget. Bill Nelson hadn't really been a handsome man, but he was so kind, so funny, that you thought he was handsome, too. He owned an ad agency called Nelson Creative that he had started with his brother, Fred. Fred was the businessman, and Bill supplied the imagination.

Natalie's dad had loved writing ads, especially funny ones. His first big campaign was some TV ads for the Brennan Furniture Company. The first ad showed a couch lying in a huge bed, and the couch was having a dream. And the couch dreamed it had wings. And the couch flew up into the sky with a dozen other couches, flying in a V like geese. And then a jet flew by. And the camera followed the jet, and inside the jet, instead of airplane seats, there were rows of Brennan couches with people looking very comfortable. And the punch line was "Stop dreaming. Fly Brennan." The ads were a big hit, and Brennan couches flew out of furniture stores all around the country. And from then on, companies lined up to have Bill Nelson at Nelson Creative make people feel good about their products.

Of course, Zoe hadn't known all that. All she knew was how much Natalie loved her dad, and how hard it was for her to lose him. That was when they were in second grade. About four months after the accident Natalie came for a sleepover at her house. And at bedtime, Zoe's dad came into her room to tuck them in. He bent over and gave Zoe a kiss good night, and at that moment Zoe looked over at Natalie. Zoe never forgot the look on Natalie's face—angry and soft and hurt and strong all at the same time. Zoe had been careful ever since not to talk about the good times she had with her dad. She didn't want to hurt her friend.

And now, four years later, when she read Natalie's book, Zoe saw things. Not about the girl in the book, because Angela wasn't much like Natalie at all. It wasn't that part. It was when the girl's father got involved in the story. Because it was the girl's father who stood by Angela all the way through. Even when the girl got caught cheating, her dad didn't give up on her. He saw she was alone, and he stepped in. The father knew the cheating had to be about something else. And when the school came down hard on Angela in the story, it was the dad who took on the headmaster and the administration. And the way he did it—by showing how the school had been cheating everyone, all the kids and the teachers, too—made Angela's dad the hero.

When Natalie talked about her book, she said the story was about Angela and her friends. But

Zoe knew there was more to it. It was about a girl and her dad. The book was like a good-bye poem from Natalie to her father.

That's why Zoe spent the weekend thinking and planning. Getting the book published would be good for Natalie, and good for her mom, too.

And by Monday morning Zoe had her ducks all in a row.

CHAPTER 9

The Agent

Zoe was waiting at the curb in front of the school when Natalie got out of her taxi on Monday morning. Her first look into Natalie's face told Zoe everything: Cassandra Day was dead again.

With a little too much forced cheerfulness in her voice Zoe said, "Hi, Nat. Get some good writing done over the weekend?"

Natalie pressed her lips together, shook her head, and frowned. She stepped around Zoe and went up the front steps.

Zoe was right behind her. "Come on, Natalie. Don't give up. I've got a whole new idea, a really good one."

Just inside the glass doors Natalie turned around. "Listen, can we just stop talking about this? I'm sorry I ever showed you my stupid story. So let's just forget about it, okay?" But Natalie knew better, even as she was saying the words. Asking Zoe to stop something halfway was like asking a chimp to lay off the bananas.

Zoe was all business. "Are you done pouting now? Because I've got something important to say. I talked with my dad, and I did some thinking, and all Cassandra Day needs is a good agent. You know what an agent is?"

Natalie heaved a sigh and shrugged off her backpack, letting it thump onto the floor behind her. "Yes, I know what an agent is. And I talked with my mom, so I also know that it's almost as hard to get an agent for a book as it is to get a book published."

"Well, what would you say if I told you that I've already got you an agent?"

"You're kidding, right?" said Natalie.

"Not kidding," said Zoe.

"So . . . who is it?" Natalie was cautious but interested, even a little flattered.

Zoe smiled. "Okay, her name is Sherry Clutch,

and she's known my dad for more than ten years, and thanks to me, she knows all about your story, and she's really interested . . . even if the book's not completely finished yet."

Natalie narrowed her eyes and looked sideways at Zoe. "So, what's the catch? There's got to be a catch."

"No, really. There's no catch . . . except—"

"Aha!" Natalie cut in. "Except what? Sounds like a catch to me. C'mon, out with it."

Zoe went on, "Well . . . you know how you're Cassandra Day? Well, Sherry Clutch . . . she's me! Get it? I'm your agent!"

Natalie's face was a dictionary of emotions. Horror. Disbelief. Disappointment. Then anger. She grabbed her backpack, wheeled around, and started up the stairs. "That's not funny, Zoe. It's not funny at all."

Again Zoe was at her heels. "But listen, Nat. I can do this, I really can. An agent is just someone who works for a writer. It's just a person who really believes a writer is great. I know your book is good. I know I can get your mom to take it seriously. It's gonna get a fair shot, I know it!"

Natalie didn't stop and she didn't turn

around. She turned left at the first corridor and headed for her locker, taking long purposeful strides. Zoe sprinted ahead, turned, and planted herself in Natalie's path. Natalie was a whole head taller, and Zoe half expected to be knocked over.

But Natalie stopped. Jaw clenched and eyes hard, she looked down into Zoe's face.

Zoe said, "Please, Natalie. Just let me give it a try. It'll be fun, and I know I can do this . . . I *know* I can. And don't you think Sherry Clutch is just *the* most perfect name for an agent?"

Part of Natalie just wanted to push right past this girl and never talk to her again. But her training as a writer stopped her. In a fraction of a second, in that way that writers do, she took a mental step back and considered the scene before her. There was Zoe. Ridiculous? Yes, but also completely loyal, completely enthusiastic, completely confident. Here they stood in the hall, face-to-face. Dozens of kids streamed by in both directions, lockers slammed, laughter and shouts and noise rose all around them. And in that instant Natalie saw what mattered. It wasn't whether the book got published or not.

It wasn't whether Zoe was absolutely crazy—which she was. The important thing was Zoe herself, her friend.

So Natalie had to roll her eyes and smile. She had to. And then she put out her hand and shook Zoe's. Then in her author's voice Natalie said, "Ms. Clutch, I'm Cassandra Day. My friend Zoe says you're a terrific agent. Can you tell me a little about yourself?"

In bits and pieces during their morning classes Zoe told Natalie about her plans. Natalie had to admit they were impressive—crazy, but still impressive. Except that, as usual, Zoe wanted to do everything herself.

But during lunch Natalie said, "It all sounds good, Zoe, but I want to have Ms. Clayton read my book too. She might have some ideas about how to get it published."

Zoe looked hurt. "Ms. Clayton? What does she know?"

Natalie shrugged. "I don't know. That's what I want to find out."

"But I've already thought of everything."

Natalie narrowed her eyes. "Everything? I

don't think so. I mean, like, look at this." Natalie pointed at the piece of stationery that Zoe had designed and printed up on her computer at home over the weekend. "Zoe, I hate to tell you, but this stationery doesn't look real."

"I know," said Zoe. "It's just the prototype. I'll take it to a Kwik Kopy and have fifty sheets printed up on nice paper."

Natalie said, "That's not what I mean." She pointed at the top of the page, below where it said SHERRY CLUTCH LITERARY AGENCY. "Look. There's no office address, there's no phone number, no E-mail address, no fax number. No one's going to believe this."

Zoe gave Natalie one of her Do-you-really-think-I'm-that-dumb? kinds of looks. She patted Natalie's arm and said, "Trust me. I've got it all figured out, I really do. That's my job, remember? But if it'll make you feel better to have Ms. Clayton get involved, then fine. That'll be fine. I'll figure that out too. All *you* have to do is finish the book and leave the rest to me."

Natalie wished it could actually be that simple, but she knew better. With Zoe in charge, nothing was simple.

CHAPTER 10

The Chosen Grown-Up

LAURA CLAYTON

Laura Clayton sorted the remains of her lunch into the recycling bins in the teachers' room—glass, paper, plastic. As she rinsed her salad container she caught a glimpse of herself in the mirror above the sink. She looked exhausted. It was her second year of teaching, and it was January, and Laura Clayton had to keep reminding herself that she loved her job.

Ms. Clayton glanced up at the clock, then opened the hallway door and walked briskly toward her classroom. She didn't feel prepared for sixth period. She never felt prepared for sixth period. It was her most challenging group of kids, and the hour between twelve thirty and one thirty was when her daily energy level hit rock bottom.

Nothing—not her own years in New York's best private schools, not her bachelor's degree from Barnard College, not her master's degree from Bank Street College, not even her student teaching—nothing had prepared her for the daily grind of classroom teaching, and especially teaching her sixth-grade class on a Monday afternoon.

The Deary School emphasized writing, and Laura Clayton agreed wholeheartedly. The curriculum required at least three writing assignments per week. Again, Ms. Clayton agreed. Writing was a vital skill. But she taught five English classes a day to grades five through eight. Even though Ms. Clayton's average class size was only thirteen students, if she gave a simple, one-paragraph writing assignment to each kid, that meant at least four hours of reading and commenting and evaluating for her.

A group of Laura's friends from Barnard College still lived in the city, and they couldn't understand why she wouldn't go out to clubs and shows with them on weeknights anymore. They had jobs at places like banks and ad agencies, department stores and publishing companies—one of her friends even worked at the United Nations. They had jobs where a person could slide by on four hours of sleep once in a while. Ms. Clayton had tried teaching five English classes on four hours of sleep once or twice. Now she knew better.

The sound of chirping robins came from the speaker below the clock in Ms. Clayton's room. That was the class-passing sound for February. Four years back the new headmaster had replaced the bell timers with a programmable sound system. So far this year the passing sounds had been a humpback whale song, the honking of migrating geese, a bouncing basketball, the sound of bamboo wind chimes, and a Mozart flute solo.

The old alarm bell was gone, but chirping birds had the same effect. Kids burst from their walled containers all over the school, and for seven minutes a cheerful chaos shook both buildings of the Deary School. Then the sound of chirping robins—played much louder for the start-of-class signal—magically guided each student to the doorway of another walled container. For fourteen of the sixth graders at the Deary School that meant English class in the Linden Room. Ms. Clayton braced herself, and sixth period began.

Fifty-three minutes later robins chirped again in the Linden Room. Ms. Clayton handed out an assignment sheet explaining how to write a short persuasive essay, and then she dismissed the class. The kids left the room heading for their exercise period, and Ms. Clayton picked up an eraser and began clearing the chalkboard. As she methodically swept the board clean she took stock. Overall it had been a pretty decent class. They had read editorials on the same subject from three different news magazines. They had identified the persuasive words and techniques of each writer. The discussion had been lively but not too unruly, and the students did most of the talking. All in all, it had been a very good session. And now she had a full hour before her last class of the day. Another Monday was almost over.

When Ms. Clayton finished erasing the board and turned around, Zoe and Natalie were standing beside her desk.

Ms. Clayton said, "Yes, girls? What is it?"

As arranged, Natalie spoke first. "Ms. Clayton, Zoe and I want to start a writing club, and we were wondering if you could be our adviser."

Ms. Clayton smiled at them and sat down in her chair. "A writing club? You mean like creative writing?"

Natalie nodded. "Yeah, that's right. Creative writing."

Ms. Clayton was pleased. Natalie was a talented writer, easily better than any of her other students, even the kids in grades seven and eight. No matter what writing assignment she gave, Natalie Nelson's work always stood out.

She turned to Zoe. Zoe's writing was all right, but it was nothing like Natalie's. Ms. Clayton said, "And you, Zoe? You want to be in the writing club too?"

Zoe said, "Oh, yes, I do."

"And do you want to invite students from the upper grades to join," asked Ms. Clayton, "or were you just thinking of having it be a sixth-grade club?"

Zoe said, "Well . . . really we were hoping that it could be just me and Natalie in the club. 'Cause . . . well, we want it to be more like a . . . like a publishing club."

Ms. Clayton's eyebrows went up. "A publishing club?"

"Yeah," said Zoe, "because, you see, well, I mean, you know how Natalie's a great writer? Well, you see, she's almost done with her first novel, and it's a really great novel—it's really, really good—and, and . . . Natalie's book has got to get published. It's . . . it's *got* to. So, really we want to start a publishing club. Like I said."

"A . . . publishing . . . club." Ms. Clayton was having trouble getting her mind around the idea.

Zoe nodded. "Uh-huh. Natalie's the writer, I'm her agent, and you . . . you're our adviser. You help us. You help us get Natalie's book published. So it's a publishing club."

Both girls stood waiting. Natalie was blushing, looking down at her feet, embarrassed. Not Zoe.

Zoe leaned forward, both her hands on the teacher's desk, looking at Ms. Clayton's face.

Ms. Clayton didn't know what to say. It made sense, in a sixth-grade sort of way. But somehow—she wasn't quite sure why—it felt like trouble. She was just about to start shaking her head, just about to start making excuses, just about to say, "No thanks," when Zoe reached into her backpack, pulled out Natalie's manuscript, and laid it on the desk.

Zoe said, "Well, we've got to run to gym now, so we'll come and talk to you tomorrow before school. And here's the manuscript. You should read it—it's really good. See you tomorrow."

As the robins began chirping from the speaker below the clock, Zoe took Natalie's hand and pulled her toward the doorway.

And Ms. Clayton gave them a wave and a half-dazed little smile and said, "Yes . . . fine. See you tomorrow."

CHAPTER 11

welcome to
the club

Laura Clayton sat at her desk. The school had slowly become silent in the late afternoon, but she had not noticed. She had been reading. And now she was done.

Zoe had told the truth. "The Cheater," by Natalie Nelson, was a remarkable novel. Ms. Clayton had read part of the manuscript during her free period, right after Zoe put it on her desk. After school she sat down at her desk again and didn't move until she'd finished the last page. Like Zoe, Ms. Clayton couldn't wait to read the rest of the book.

The novel was intense, but it was also funny. Ms. Clayton had been pulled into the lives of four friends at a private school in New York. The plot was clever, and the book also explored some big ideas, like loyalty and friendship, and learning the difference between right and wrong.

There was one passage that really got her, close to the end. It was when the girl watched her dad. He was inside the headmaster's office, and she was outside, watching him through a glass wall.

My father sits and listens politely to Dr. Sipes. Dr. Sipes is doing his best to send me to a special school, a school for problem kids. I don't need to hear his words. I can read his face. He wants to make an example of me. It's not about me. It's about his rules. It's about keeping his school under control. I can see all this in his face.

Dr. Sipes stands up and paces now, but he stays behind his desk, always behind his desk. The desk is a barrier. It is a drawbridge. It is the moat of his castle. He hides there. When he stays behind his desk, he feels safe.

Suddenly my father stands too. I am seeing the side of his face. He shakes his head no. He will not hear these bad things. Not about me. He knows better. He knows me better. My father leans forward. He leans over the desk. Dr. Sipes steps back, as if pushed by a finger on his chest.

My father has asked a question. I can see the question in the tilt of his chin. I can see the question hang there in the air above the wide desk. And I can see that it is a challenge. It is a glove tossed onto the draw-bridge.

And Dr. Sipes does not move. He cannot answer the challenge. He does not pick up the glove. It lies there smol-dering on his desk. And I can see my father has won. He has done battle. For me. And he has won.

I stand up as he comes out of the headmaster's office. My father smiles

at me, and it is like the sun coming
from behind a cloud. "Come on, Angela.
We're going home now."

   My father walks out and does not
look back.

   Neither do I.

There was a power and a depth to Natalie's writing that surprised Ms. Clayton. If the ending was anywhere near as good as the first fifteen chapters, "The Cheater" was a book Ms. Clayton would buy for herself and her classroom, and she'd also recommend it to all her friends. If she hadn't been Natalie's writing teacher for the past five months, she never would have believed a twelve-year-old had written it.

Ms. Clayton walked toward her room on Tuesday morning, bulging briefcase in one hand, coffee cup in the other. When she turned the corner on the second floor, there beside her locked door stood Natalie and Zoe.

"Good morning, Ms. Clayton," said Natalie, and Zoe waved and said, "Hi."

Ms. Clayton smiled and said, "Good morning, girls." She set her briefcase down, took a key ring from her coat pocket, and unlocked the door. Zoe pulled it open for her and then followed her into the Linden Room. Natalie hung back in the doorway, but Zoe motioned her to come in, so she did.

Ms. Clayton put her coffee on the desk, set her briefcase on her chair, and then walked over to the large wardrobe to hang up her coat and scarf. With her back to the girls, she said, "I've read the manuscript. I read it here at school yesterday, and again at home last night." Turning to look at Natalie, she smiled. "Zoe's right, Natalie. It's an excellent novel, and once you finish it, I'm almost sure someone will want to publish it."

Natalie blushed and gulped. She said, "Do you really think so?"

Ms. Clayton nodded and said, "Well, I'm no publisher, but I've read a lot of books, and I think I know a good one when I see it." Coming over to her desk, Ms. Clayton pulled the manuscript folder from her briefcase and set it on the green blotter. Then she moved her briefcase to the floor and sat down. "Pull a couple of chairs over here, and let's talk about this idea for a club."

The girls took off their coats and sat, Zoe on the left and Natalie on the right. Ms. Clayton said, "Now, since this is New York City and we know a lot of publishers are located here, we could just open up the Yellow Pages and find the addresses of three or four publishers. Then when Natalie finishes her book, we can send the manuscript to one of them . . . or maybe even to three or four at once. I'll be happy to help you figure out how to do that, and then we can wait and see what happens. Is that what you have in mind?"

Zoe shifted in her chair and said, "Well, not exactly."

Natalie said, "You see, my mom works at a publishing company, and I've been there and I've seen what happens when writers just send stuff. If we do what you said, my manuscript will just get dumped into a big pile with all the other mail."

Zoe added, "And my dad said that unless you have an agent, no one will ever read your manuscript. That's why I'm Natalie's agent."

"You're her agent?" Ms. Clayton sipped her coffee and then said, "Oh, yes—I think you said that yesterday. What else?"

Zoe sat up on the front edge of her chair, her eyes bright. "And, well, we want Natalie's mom to be the first editor to read the book, but we don't want her to know Natalie wrote it because—"

"Because you want her mom to be objective—not be influenced one way or the other, right?" said Ms. Clayton.

And Zoe said, "Right."

Then Zoe sketched out her plan. While Zoe explained, Natalie watched Ms. Clayton's face. The signs were not good.

"And that's all there is to it!" said Zoe. "So, what do you think?"

Ms. Clayton pushed her chair back from the desk a little and sat up straight. "I don't know. The pseudonym . . . and then you pretending to be Natalie's agent—that doesn't seem quite honest . . . and I'm not even sure it's legal."

Natalie kicked Zoe's chair. "See?" she said, and then turning to Ms. Clayton she added, "That's what I told Zoe. I told her that making up all these names was just like lying, and I told her I didn't want to do it."

Ms. Clayton said, "Changing *your* name isn't the part I'm concerned about, Natalie. Zoe's right. Using a pen name is perfectly acceptable, and many writers through the years have done it. The man who wrote *Alice's Adventures in Wonderland* used a pseudonym, and there was a French woman who used the name George Sand, and lots more—that part is just fine. It's Zoe pretending to be an agent—that's what worries me."

Zoe shook her head. "But I'm not pretending to be her agent. I *am* her agent. I know I'm just a kid, but does it say somewhere that an agent has to be old?"

Ms. Clayton squinted and took another sip of coffee. Then she said, "Well, most agents *are* grown-ups, but if Natalie has asked you to try to get her novel published, then . . . I guess that makes you her agent. Still, there's no such agency as this Sherry Clutch company."

Zoe said, "But don't people just make up names for their companies sometimes? You know, just make up a new name? That's okay, isn't it?"

Ms. Clayton said, "Well, yes . . . I guess so."

"So I'm making up the name of a new company—the Sherry Clutch Literary Agency," said Zoe.

Natalie said, "But you said *your* name was going to be Sherry Clutch."

Zoe gave Natalie a withering look and said, "Not if our *adviser* says it shouldn't be. If that's a problem . . . then . . . then I'll use my own name, so it'll be me contacting your mom from the Sherry Clutch Agency."

Natalie snorted. "Yeah, like my mom won't know right away that it's you."

Zoe wheeled to face Ms. Clayton. "People are allowed to have nicknames, right?"

Ms. Clayton nodded her agreement but looked puzzled.

Zoe continued, "So I'm going to use the name my grandma calls me. It's my nickname— Zee Zee. I'm going to be Zee Zee from the Sherry Clutch Agency—Zee Zee . . . *Reisman*." And when Zoe said her last name, it sounded like "raceman."

Natalie said, "Your name doesn't sound like that. It sounds like 'rice,' not like 'race.' And besides, when you sign a letter, the spelling will still be the same, and my mom will know."

Zoe snapped back, "I'm not the only Reisman in New York City, Natalie. Open up the phone book. Go ahead, take a look. Tons of people spell their name like mine. And who says I have to say my name to sound like 'riceman'? Who says? I can pronounce my name any way I want to—isn't that right, Ms. Clayton?" And Ms. Clayton, now a referee, nodded again in favor of Zoe.

Zoe was in full argument mode now. "So, here's how it works. It's okay for Natalie to become Cassandra Day, because she's an author; and it's okay to name a new company and call it the Sherry Clutch Agency; and it's okay for me to call myself Zee Zee 'Raceman,' because it's still my real name and I'm just changing it a little to protect the identity of my author. So I guess everything's okay, right?"

Zoe looked from Natalie to Ms. Clayton. Ms. Clayton looked from Zoe to Natalie. And then Natalie and Ms. Clayton both looked at Zoe. Ms. Clayton sighed and said, "I should probably get my head examined, but I have to agree with you, Zoe. I think everything you described is perfectly legal. And the novel is certainly real, so it's not like we're trying to commit a fraud on anyone. So . . ." Ms. Clayton reached across her desk and shook Natalie's hand and then Zoe's. She smiled and said, "Ladies, I think we have a publishing club. So, what's next? Any ideas?"

Natalie said, "Ideas? That's Zoe's department— and you're going to be sorry that you ever asked."

As is turned out, Natalie was right.

CHAPTER 12

In or Out?

Now that a grown-up was involved, Natalie felt better about everything. Zoe didn't seem quite as insane, and it was exciting that Ms. Clayton liked her book. Natalie felt like she could write again. So for the rest of the week she wrote for two hours every night, and then she worked all afternoon on both Saturday and Sunday. It turned out that all the story needed was three more chapters, and by Sunday night her book was done.

Riding into the city on Monday morning, her mom said, "We didn't get to spend much time together this weekend, Nat. And you look so tired. Is it my imagination, or do you have a lot more homework lately?"

Natalie smiled and said, "Yeah, there's more homework, but I'm also doing some creative writing. That's why I've been so busy."

"Creative writing for your English class?"

Natalie paused and then said, "Well, sort of."

"Sometimes I think your English teacher goes overboard with the work. I mean, she's good, and her comments on your assignments are excellent. But still, kids shouldn't have to slave every second. I'm sorry I didn't get to your open house so I could have met her. I have half a mind to call her and tell her to lay off every once in a while."

Natalie shook her head. "No, it's not like that, Mom. This writing, it's mostly something I've been working on—on my own."

Her mom smiled. "Well, I'm glad you enjoy writing, but you really need to get enough rest. And if you have enough time to go shopping with me or go to the movies now and then, that'd be nice too."

Natalie smiled back. "Sorry, Mom. Next weekend will be different, I promise."

. . . . .

When the Publishing Club met in the Linden Room on Monday afternoon, Natalie gave a finished manuscript to Zoe and another one to Ms. Clayton. Blushing a little, she said, "I finished the book. You'll have to read it and see if the ending's any good."

Zoe hugged the stack of paper and said, "I can't wait!"

Ms. Clayton beamed and said, "Neither can I. I'm sure it's going to be great, Natalie."

And when they met again early Tuesday morning, everyone agreed that the ending was perfect. The book was done. It was time to send it to a publisher.

Now that the manuscript was ready, Zoe put her plan into high gear. At the end of English class on Tuesday afternoon Zoe handed Ms. Clayton a big brown envelope. During her free period Ms. Clayton opened it. There was a neatly typed letter from Zoe, and when she opened a separate, smaller envelope, she let out a gasp. The envelope contained five hundred dollars in cash.

Ms. Clayton began reading Zoe's letter:

```
Dear Ms. Clayton:

First of all, don't get scared about
the other envelope. I know it's a lot
of money, but it's all mine from
birthdays and holidays, and I can spend
it any way I want to. It's really mine.
So don't worry about that. Here's what
we need to do.
```

As Ms. Clayton read Zoe's detailed instructions her eyes got wider and wider.

Mr. Archer, the headmaster, happened to walk past the open doorway of the Linden Room as Ms. Clayton was reading the second page of Zoe's letter. He stopped and took a step into the room.

"Laura?" he said.

Ms. Clayton jerked her head up, saw Mr. Archer, and then slapped Zoe's letter facedown onto the envelope of money.

Mr. Archer looked concerned. He said, "Is everything all right?"

"All . . . all right?" stammered Ms. Clayton. "Oh, oh yes, everything's fine. I'm just . . . I . . . I'm just getting ready for my last class."

Mr. Archer smiled. "Sorry to startle you, but you looked as if you'd seen a ghost."

Ms. Clayton's laugh was forced and a little too shrill. "A ghost? Oh, no, I'm just a little tired, that's all. I'm fine . . . really. Just fine."

"Well, good. I'm glad you're fine." Mr. Archer started to turn, and then stopped and said, "Oh, I've been meaning to remind you— we need to talk sometime this week to set up another classroom observation. I'll put a note in your mailbox, all right?"

Ms. Clayton nodded. "That'll be fine. Thanks, Arthur."

Mr. Archer left, and Ms. Clayton turned the letter over and finished reading it. Then she went to the intercom by the door and called the office.

"Yes, what is it?" The tinny speaker made the secretary's voice sound even more nasal and harsh than it did in person. Mrs. Fratchi had been at the Deary School since the days when all the letters were typed on a manual typewriter and all the grade reports were written by hand. Of all the staff at the school, Mrs. Fratchi was the only one that Ms. Clayton hadn't learned to call by her first name, which was Edna.

"Mrs. Fratchi? This is Laura Clayton."

"I already know that. What is it, Miss Clayton?" Mrs. Fratchi didn't believe in calling anyone "Ms." To her, a woman was either a "Miss" or a "Mrs."

"Mrs. Fratchi, will you please ask Zoe Reisman to stop in and see me after school today?"

"Do you have her schedule?"

"N-no, but I know she's in the gym this period."

"Very well. I'll try to get the message to her."

"Thank you, Mrs. Fratchi."

There was no response. Mrs. Fratchi didn't believe in saying "You're welcome," either.

When Zoe showed up at the Linden Room after school, Ms. Clayton didn't mince words. She held up Zoe's letter and the envelope of money and said, "Listen, Zoe. I just don't feel right about this. You're asking me to go and spend a lot of money. You want me to rent an office and hire a receptionist and everything else, and I . . . I . . . I just don't know. Where will all of this end up?"

Zoe was unmoved. "Where will it end up? With Natalie's book getting published, that's where. And we're not really renting an office. Did you read my whole letter? We're just going to one of those instant office places. We pay three hundred fifty dollars, and for that we get to use their mailing address, and we get our own phone number and a fax number and an answering machine, and if someone calls during business hours, the reception lady answers the phone and says, 'Sherry Clutch Literary Agency, may I help you?' We only have to pay for a month at a time, and none of this is wrong. People do this all the time when they want to go into business. If I was old enough, I could do it myself—but I'm not, so that's the part that you have to do."

Ms. Clayton felt trapped. She imagined herself having to explain all this to Mr. Archer. She saw herself sitting in a heavy chair in the oak-paneled boardroom on the fifth floor, facing all the sober, frowning trustees of the Deary School. She imagined being charged with unprofessional behavior and never being able to teach again.

She gave a little smile and said, "I know what you're asking me to do, Zoe, but I'd feel so much better if I could talk to your parents about it. In fact, don't you think you should ask *them* to help you do all this? Why not get them involved?"

Zoe pressed her lips together. "I'm *not* getting my parents involved, because when you get parents involved, they take over—at least that's what mine would do. This is something that Natalie and I want to do on our own. If we got my dad or my mom into it, then it wouldn't be like doing it ourselves, that's all. It just wouldn't be. And we came to you because, well . . . because you're nice. And smart."

Zoe paused for about five seconds, and then she said, "But if you don't want to be our adviser, that's okay. I mean, Natalie thought you would be the best one, and so did I. But if you don't think you can help us, then I guess we'll have to ask someone else." Zoe paused again and then said, "I think Mr. Karswell might help us, don't you?"

Ms. Clayton saw what Zoe was doing. Zoe was calling her a coward, and she was saying that Mr. Karswell wouldn't be. And Zoe was probably right. Mr. Karswell taught social studies. He had been at the school for about five years, and he had a reputation for being sort of a rebel. He was the editor of the school newspaper, and he coached the varsity soccer team. He was always bursting with energy, and he ran in the New York Marathon every fall, and last summer he had paddled his kayak up the Hudson River all the way to the Adirondack Mountains. And on top of all that, he was good looking. Sooner or later almost every girl at the Deary School got a crush on Mr. Karswell. Even Ms. Clayton.

Ms. Clayton blushed. Zoe had cut off every possible escape. If she backed out now, she would brand herself a coward. And she was not a coward. Even if she had never run a marathon.

Ms. Clayton was learning the same lesson that Zoe's older sisters had learned years ago: to argue is to lose.

Forty-five minutes later Laura Clayton was sitting at a small desk in the reception area of

Offices Unlimited, filling out paperwork.

Name of Business: _Sherry Clutch Litsrary Agency_

Nature of Business: _author rspressntation_

Renter's Name: _Laura S. Clayton_

Term of Rental: _x_ monthly _____ yearly

That part of the form was simple. It was all simple, just like Zoe had said it would be. Zoe had done her research well.

Then Ms. Clayton checked off the services Zoe had asked for:

REQUIRED SERVICES:

_x_ phone answering _x_ voice-mail service _x_ beeper _x_ fax receiving

___ E-mail _x_ postal service ___ stenographic service ___ messenger service

___ Federal Express service ___ desktop computer ___ laptop computer

___ Internet access ___ office space, furnished ___ office space, unfurnished

There was a lot of fine print at the bottom of the form, and then a line for a signature. Laura paused, then took a deep breath, signed the sheet, and stood up to hand it across the counter to the office manager. The young woman calculated the first month's rent, then looked up and said, "That'll be three hundred forty-seven dollars and seventy-five cents. How will you be paying today?"

Laura opened her purse and started to reach for Zoe's cash, then had a flash of inspiration. Instead of Zoe's money she grabbed her own billfold, opened it, and pulled out her MasterCard. She handed it to the lady. "I'll be using this, thanks."

Instantly Ms. Clayton felt so much better. Maybe helping the girls was a crazy idea, and maybe she shouldn't be doing it at all, but at least she could keep every bit of Zoe's cash safe and sound. No one would be able to accuse her of wasting the money of a poor, defenseless child. Thinking of Zoe as "a poor, defenseless child" almost made Ms. Clayton burst out laughing.

Three minutes later the office manager handed Ms. Clayton four things: a small black beeper; a sheet that listed the new phone number, the new fax number, and the mailing address; a separate sheet that told "How to Record Your Company's Outgoing Voice-Mail Message," "How to Call and Retrieve Your Voice-Mail," and "How to Use Your Beeper." The fourth thing she gave Ms. Clayton was a receipt for the payment.

Offices Unlimited was on upper Broadway, only about five blocks from Ms. Clayton's apartment. So on her way home she stopped at her bank and opened a new savings account. She deposited $347.75 of Zoe's cash. Ms. Clayton tucked the new passbook into the bottom of her purse. Then she put the receipt for the office in the envelope with the leftover money. That way, when she gave Zoe the envelope, it would look like she had used the cash to pay for the office.

Walking up Broadway with a spring in her step, Ms. Clayton felt alive, energized. The smell of pizza mixed with the exhaust from the 104 bus, and the streetlights seemed bright and cheery in the gathering dusk. As she turned right onto Ninety-eighth Street, Ms. Clayton thought about what she'd just done—the office, the money, the beeper, the new savings account. And she smiled. She was glad she hadn't sent Zoe and Natalie looking for another adviser. She thought, *I did it! The Sherry Clutch Literary Agency is ready for action. I am Ms. Clayton the Fearless, Ms. Clayton the Bold!*

Then after another ten steps she thought, *Yeah, right. Who am I kidding? I'm the slightly wacky Ms. Clayton, that's who I am. But whatever happens, I'm going to be right in the middle of it—and it's going to be an adventure!*

CHAPTER 13

Open for Business

By Friday afternoon everything was set.

Zoe had put all the right numbers on the Sherry Clutch stationery, and she had had fifty sheets printed up on good-quality paper at a Kwik Kopy shop on Lexington Avenue. She'd also had twenty-five large self-stick address labels printed.

Natalie made some last-minute changes to her novel and then printed two double-spaced copies of the manuscript, one for the publisher and one to keep for herself. The manuscript was ninety-seven pages, and the title page said:

The Cheater

by Cassandra Day

Looking at it gave Natalie goose bumps.

The first phone call to Hannah Nelson would be important, and Zoe was worried.

Zoe and Natalie were in gym class on Friday afternoon. Zoe said, "So, when I call your mom today, she's got to say it's okay for me to send her the manuscript, and then when she gets it, she's got to want to read it." Zoe was quiet for a minute. Then she said, "My dad told me that when you want a person to agree with you, never ask a question they can answer by saying no. But I don't get how to do that, do you?"

Natalie shook her head and shrugged. They were both quiet, sitting on a rolled-up tumbling mat, waiting for their turn on the balance beam.

Then Natalie had an idea. She said, "How about if you don't talk to her at all?"

Zoe said, "What do you mean?"

And when Natalie told her, Zoe nodded and said, "Of course! That's it! Why didn't I think of that?"

Natalie grinned and said, "Because sometimes brilliant writers have to help their stupid agents, that's why."

· · · · ·

By 3:10 the Deary School had gotten pretty quiet. At exactly 3:15 Natalie called her mom from the pay phone on the wall outside the office.

"Hannah Nelson."

"Hi, Mom, it's me. I'm still at school, so I'm going to be a little late. How's your day going?"

As soon as her mom answered, Natalie turned and gave a thumbs-up to Ms. Clayton, who was watching from down the hall. Ms. Clayton walked briskly to the Linden Room, stuck her head inside the door, and said, "Okay, Zoe. Natalie's talking to her mom."

Zoe sat down at Ms. Clayton's desk and quickly dialed seven numbers on her cell phone, then pushed the Send button. Ten seconds later she heard Natalie's mom's voice: "You've reached Hannah Nelson at Shipley Junior Books. I'm on another call or away from my desk right now. Please leave your name and number after the tone and I'll call you back."

Zoe had practiced her agent voice for the past two days, driving Natalie nuts with it. Zoe always talked fast anyway, but Zee Zee talked even faster. Zee Zee's voice was also deeper, but most of all it was louder. Zoe had decided that Zee Zee should be loud.

So after the beep on the voice mail Zee Zee jumped right into her prepared message. Ms. Clayton stood guard in the hallway outside the Linden Room, and she could hear Zoe's performance right through the door: "Hannah—this is Zee Zee Reisman from the Sherry Clutch Agency? Listen, I've got this terrific manuscript by an author named Cassandra Day. You've got to read this. I've got a messenger bringing it to your

office this afternoon. You really have to read this. Even though this is her first novel, I know a lot of editors will be interested, but Cassandra wanted Shipley to see it first because she likes a lot of the other books

you've done there. I'm in and out a lot, but you can phone me at 212-555-8878. If I'm not in, the office will beep me. Let me know what you think as soon as you can, 'cause like I said, this is a hot one. Thanks a lot—bye."

Zoe's heart was racing as she hung up the phone.

Ms. Clayton walked back to the corner of the hallway and waved to Natalie. Natalie ended her talk with her mom by saying, "Well, I'll be leaving in a few minutes, so I'll be there in about half an hour or so."

Her mom said, "No need to hurry. I'd like to get out of here early this afternoon, but I don't think it's going to happen. Letha's on the warpath, and my phone's been ringing all day long. So bring your homework, honey. See you soon."

· · · · ·

Natalie got off the elevator at Shipley Junior Books at 4:25. She walked to the desk and handed a thick brown envelope to the receptionist. Natalie smiled and said, "A messenger brought this—it's for my mom. Do you need to check it in, or can I take it right back to her?"

He looked at the address label and said, "All it needs is a date stamp and my initials." The stamp made a mechanical *ca-chonk* sound as he pressed it onto the front of the envelope, and then he scribbled his initials below the date. Now the package looked official. "Here you go." He handed the envelope back to Natalie, then pushed the security button to open the door for her.

Natalie wound her way through the maze to her mom's office. Her mouth was dry. Even though she'd been here a hundred times, she felt like a spy sneaking into a strange building.

"Hi, Mom."

As her mom swung her chair around and smiled, Natalie glanced at the phone console on the desk beside the computer screen. The Message Waiting light was dark. That meant her mom had already listened to Zee Zee's message.

"Here," Natalie said, and she handed the envelope to her mom. "This is for you."

Hannah Nelson looked at the envelope. The large address label was printed in bright green ink. She read the return address aloud. "'The Sherry Clutch Literary Agency'? I just had a message from this agent, but I don't think I know her. . . . Oh, well." And she dropped the envelope onto the papers beside her computer. "Could you get me a juice or something, Natalie? I didn't even stop for lunch today."

Natalie returned with two bottles of apple juice and some shortbread cookies. Her mom held up her bottle for a toast, and when Natalie clinked it, her mom said, "Here's to our weekend!"

And at that moment Letha walked in. She stepped across the space carefully and leaned over to look at Hannah's computer screen. Natalie caught the sharp scent of Letha's perfume and took a step backward.

With a strained smile Letha said, "I love the weekend too, but I don't think it's quite here yet. Have you double-checked all those revisions, Hannah? The production manager is calling me for that text every half hour, and we

Shipley Junior Books

Letha Springfield

EDITOR IN CHIEF

can't get out of here until it's released."

Glancing around Hannah's workspace, she snatched up the new envelope and said, "What's this?"

Hannah said, "That? It's just a manuscript. Must be a new agency—Sherry something."

Letha read the label. "Sherry Clutch . . . oh, yes, I believe I've heard of her. She's supposed to be very bright. Listen—buzz me the second you're sure all those revisions check out, okay? And I want you to give this a look over the weekend." Letha dropped the envelope on Hannah's lap and swept out of the office.

Hannah shook her head and gave Natalie a wry smile. "So much for the weekend, eh?

Listen, I've got to get back to work. Tim is probably gone by now, so you can hang out over there, okay?"

Natalie said, "Sure, Mom."

As she walked over to Tim's cubicle, Natalie tried not to smile. The editorial director of Shipley Junior Books had just pretended that she knew all about the Sherry Clutch Literary Agency. And then she had ordered her best editor to read a novel written by a twelve-year-old.

Alone in Tim's office, Natalie grinned. For the first time ever she was glad that her mom's boss was a fire-breathing, stuck-up know-it-all.

CHAPTER 14

Judgment Day

After Letha told her mom to read the manuscript, Cassandra Day couldn't wait to tell her agent about this unexpected development.

Natalie actually picked up the phone in Tim's office and dialed half of Zoe's number. Then she stopped and said to herself, *Do I really want Zoe calling me every five minutes all weekend long asking me, "Has she read it? Has she read it yet?"* Natalie hung up the phone.

Then she picked it up and dialed the number again. Zoe deserved some kind of a progress report. *But she doesn't need to know everything—bad enough that one of us has to worry the whole weekend.*

"Zoe Reisman's room at the Reisman residence, Zoe Reisman speaking."

Natalie kept her voice low because her mom's office was only about ten feet away. "Zoe? It's me. The manuscript is here. It's in my mom's office."

Zoe was excited. "Great! Is she going to read it? Did she listen to my message? Do you think she suspects anything?"

"I know she got your message, and she doesn't suspect a thing. And I'm pretty sure she's going to read it. So we'll just have to see what happens next."

"You know," said Zoe slowly, "you could maybe help things along. You know, like pick up the envelope and say, 'I wonder if this one's any good'—something like that."

Natalie smiled, but she talked in a serious voice. She wanted Zoe to calm down. "No, I think we better just let things move ahead on their own. If there's no action in a week or so, then maybe you can call her again."

Zoe did not like that idea. "A week? Are you crazy? A week is forever! If I don't hear from her in three days, then I'm going to turn the heat up—way up!"

"Look, Zee Zee, relax. I've got to get off the phone now, but I'll let you know if anything else happens, okay?"

Zoe said, "Hey! Maybe you could offer to read it for her—you know, help out around the office?"

"Zoe?" said Natalie. "No. No, no, no. Just be patient."

"Yeah," said Zoe, "easy for you to say."

"No, it isn't easy for me to say, Zoe. I want to know what she thinks about it as much as you do. But we're just going to have to let it move along one step at a time, okay?"

There was a pause, and then Zoe said, "Okay. You're right . . . I guess."

"I'll call you if there's any news, I promise."

"Okay," said Zoe. "Bye."

When they finally left the office at seven-fifteen on Friday night, Natalie could see the envelope from the Sherry Clutch Literary Agency sticking up from the outside pocket of her mom's briefcase.

Natalie tried to think. She tried to decide what she was feeling. She couldn't figure out if she was happy or scared or numb or what. Because what Zoe had said at the very beginning was true now. All of a sudden her mom wasn't just her mom. She was her editor. Hannah Nelson would be the first person to read "The Cheater" in a professional way. Her own mom would be comparing Natalie's story to all the other manuscripts she had read during the past five years at Shipley Junior Books—manuscripts written by successful, established, professional authors. Part of Natalie wanted to snatch that envelope out of her mom's briefcase and toss it into a trash barrel. But it was too late for that. The day of judgment had arrived.

But that day wasn't Friday. Friday night when they got home, Natalie and her mom went right out again and ate at a Chinese restaurant and then caught a late movie at the local theater— one of those British movies where half the actors wear fancy clothes and the other half look like beggars. It was a lively story with plenty of action and a little bit of romance, but Natalie couldn't stay focused on it. Her mind kept wandering back to that envelope, still in the briefcase, sitting on a chair in the entryway of their loft.

And Saturday wasn't judgment day either. In the morning they went grocery shopping, and then there was the laundry, and then they both spent two hours cleaning the loft from one end to the other. And then it was dinnertime.

Natalie went to her room to read after dinner, hoping that if she left her mom alone, she'd remember the manuscript. At about nine o'clock Natalie opened her bedroom door and walked softly toward the living-room area. Peeking from behind the big, leafy plants that framed the living room, she saw her mom. She was asleep on the couch, feet propped up on the coffee table, open magazine on her lap, bathed in flickering light from the muted TV.

Lying in bed later, Natalie tossed and turned. She thought about the heap of envelopes stacked up in Ella's darkened office. For every envelope there was a person somewhere, and Natalie knew how each of them felt. Those people were out there tonight, sleeping in hundreds of different beds in hundreds of different towns in dozens of different states. Every day each person woke up and thought, "Maybe the editor will read my story today," or "Maybe the editor will call me today." Every day each writer wondered if the mail would bring a letter, maybe good news from New York City.

And Natalie felt guilty. *Her* envelope wasn't in a heap somewhere in a dark office. Her story was in the editor's briefcase. The editor's boss had assigned *her* story as homework.

Natalie sat up in bed and looked at the clock. It was almost midnight. She groped for the phone on her bed stand and punched the glowing buttons.

Zoe answered on the third ring, groggy and grumpy. "Hello?"

"It's me, Zoe. I've got to tell you what happened."

It took Natalie about two minutes to tell Zoe how her story found its way home with the editor for the weekend.

Zoe was wide awake now. "So she read it? Did she like it? What did she say when she finished it? C'mon, tell me, tell me!"

"Well . . . she hasn't read it . . . not yet."

"She hasn't read it? So why did you call me in the middle of the night?"

Natalie hesitated. "Because . . . because I feel

bad. I feel like the girl in my book. I feel like I'm a cheater too. All those other stories at my mom's office, stories that she'll never even look at? And here's my story, and it's all the way up at the head of the line. It just doesn't feel fair. That's all."

"Not fair? Who said things are fair? It's never fair, Natalie. You're a great writer, and someone like me isn't—is that fair? Is it?

"Well . . . no. I guess not," said Natalie. "But you're great at things I stink at."

"Exactly," said Zoe. "It all evens out. It seems unfair, but it's not. Your mom is a good editor at a good publishing company, and someone else's mom isn't. Is that fair?"

"No . . . not really."

"Of course it's not fair. It's just the way it is. Didn't you have to work hard to write your book—just as hard as those other writers did?"

Natalie nodded as she answered. "Yeah, I did. I worked hard."

"So do you know why your book is going to get looked at and some of those other ones aren't? It's because you are who you are, and your mom is who she is, and you worked hard to write a great book."

Zoe paused to let that sink in. Then she said, "And there's another reason your book will get published and most of those others won't."

Natalie asked, "Why's that?"

In her best agent voice Zoe said, "Because you have a great agent, and those other schnooks don't! Now listen, Cassandra. I'm giving you good advice, you hear me? You hang up now and get a good night's sleep. And just stop thinking so much. You artists are all alike—thinking, thinking, thinking! Not to worry, darling. Zee Zee is going to take good care of you."

After hanging up, Natalie felt better, but it still took her another hour to get to sleep.

And even after her lecture to Cassandra, Zee Zee lay awake doing some thinking of her own.

Then on Sunday it happened. It was late in the afternoon, and after finishing her math and English, Natalie settled into her beanbag chair to read about ancient Egypt in her social studies book. The chair was so comfortable, and she had stayed up too late the night before. The next thing Natalie knew, her mom was shaking her awake.

"Natalie, you won't believe this! You know this manuscript Letha made me bring home? Well, I opened it up, you know, just so I could tell her I looked at it? And I started reading it, and it's just . . . well, I couldn't stop reading! It's one of the best things I've read in a long time—and besides that, it's even a school story! Isn't that great?"

Natalie wanted to throw her arms around her mom's neck and burst into tears. She wanted to say, "It's mine, Mom! I wrote that! I wrote it for you, and I wrote it for Dad, and I'm so happy that you like it!"

But she couldn't, so she didn't. Instead Natalie gulped, and she smiled and said, "That's great, Mom. So, it's really good?"

Her mom nodded excitedly. "It's got such a wonderful feeling all through it . . . I mean, it needs some work here and there, but this Cassandra Day—that's the author—it's her first novel, and for a first novel it's terrific. I can't wait for you to read it."

And Natalie nodded and said, "I'd love to."

But as she walked back to her workroom Hannah wished she hadn't said anything to

Natalie about the book. Because the strongest section of the book was the part about this girl and her dad.

Hannah worried about Natalie. Ever since she lost her dad, Natalie had kept much more to herself. She seemed happy enough, and she didn't seem to need to talk about not having a dad, but maybe that was a problem. Hannah was glad that Fred made the effort to be part of the family, and she knew that Natalie loved him. But having an uncle who loved you wasn't the same. Nothing could ever be the same.

Hannah shook off the fear. *After all*, she thought, *isn't that why I love my work? That's the whole idea of a good book, right? It's supposed to hit you where you live. That's the point.*

Which was easy for her to see as an editor.

But seeing it as a mom was a different story.

CHAPTER 15

A New Island

Natalie and Zoe burst into Ms. Clayton's room right before first bell on Monday morning. Breathless, Zoe said, "Guess what? Natalie's mom got the manuscript, and her boss made her read it over the weekend, and her mom read it, and—she *loves* it! Isn't that terrific? We did it!"

Natalie nodded. "It's true, just like Zoe said! My mom raved about it last night, and she even mentioned it again this morning—I think she really wants to publish it!"

Ms. Clayton smiled and reached out to take both girls' hands, swept up in the excitement. "This is wonderful! And she doesn't have any idea that her own daughter wrote it—this is just too *cool*!" Then Ms. Clayton caught herself, and in her teacher voice she said, "Well, I think you both should be very proud. Neither one of you could have done it without the other."

"Or without you," said Natalie.

Ms. Clayton blushed and said, "Well, anyway, things are jumping now, aren't they? Keep me posted, and let me know if I can help, okay?" Robins started chirping, so Zoe and Natalie rushed out of the Linden Room to go to their lockers and get ready for morning meeting.

Alone, Ms. Clayton shook her head and smiled, half amused, half worried. She wished she could be twelve again. Back then all she would have seen was the fun of a moment like this. But she was twenty-six, and she was supposed to be the mature, grown-up teacher. And there were probably dangers ahead. There were still plenty of things that could go wrong with this little publishing adventure. If things started to turn sour, Ms. Clayton the Bold could easily be renamed. And her new name just might be Ms. Clayton the Idiot.

In science class Zoe was trying to pour exactly thirty cubic centimeters of distilled water into a graduated cylinder. Natalie was watching her, and all of a sudden Zoe started spilling water all over the lab table. It splashed onto Natalie's notebook, and she said, "Hey! Watch out!"

Behind her safety goggles Zoe's eyes were as big as golf balls. She slammed the water bottle down on the table and grabbed at the belt of her skirt. She pushed something into Natalie's hand, and it lay there jiggling. Zoe hissed, "It's the beeper! It's ringing! That's the silent ring—when it vibrates!"

Natalie turned the beeper and looked at the display. "Look!" she whispered, pointing it at Zoe. "Look! It's my mom's number! My editor is calling my agent!"

When lunchtime finally arrived, Zoe and Natalie ate in about six minutes and then hurried to the library. Mr. Levy was at lunch, and two eighth graders, a boy and a girl, were in charge. They were flirting with each other at the front desk, and they didn't even look up as two sixth-grade girls hurried to the back of the room and went into the foreign language booth and shut the door. Natalie sat down at one of the stations and put on a set of headphones. She opened her Spanish book, but she didn't start a tape. Zoe sat down at the workstation opposite Natalie, away from the glass wall and completely hidden by a study carrel. She quickly dug her cell phone out of her backpack. She had already entered the voice-mail number at Offices Unlimited into her speed dialer, so in ten seconds she was listening to the message.

Natalie said, "What'd she say?"

"Shhh!" hissed Zoe. "I'm still listening!"

The fifteen seconds that followed seemed like years to Natalie.

Then Zoe passed her the phone over the top of the carrel. "Here—push the star button quick, and the message will replay!"

Natalie glanced over her shoulder to be sure the eighth graders weren't looking, then pushed the star button and slipped the slim cell phone under the headphone cup covering her right ear. It was her mom's voice.

"Zee Zee? This is Hannah Nelson at Shipley Junior Books. I read the manuscript you sent me this weekend, and I think we may be interested in it. I can't say for sure just yet, but I'd appreciate it if you'd let me respond before you start sending it to any other publishers. It's certainly not perfect, but I think the flaws are manageable, and it might just fit in with our program. So, if you'd give me a call at 555-9091, we can talk about it. Again, that's 555-9091. Good-bye."

Zoe took the phone back and turned it off. Her eyes sparkled, and she said, "Great, eh? She wants to talk."

Natalie frowned and pulled off the headphones. "But it sounds like she doesn't like it as much anymore. Do you think she's changing her mind about it?"

Zoe made a face. "Of course not, silly. It's just business. She's not going to tell me that she loves it, because then I'd make her pay more money for it. She's just playing it cool. And she's afraid I'm going to show it to other publishers, because then she'd have some competition for it."

Natalie said, "But we don't want some other publisher."

Zoe smiled. "*I* know that, and *you* know that, but *she* doesn't know that—and that's good. That way, we'll get a better deal."

Natalie narrowed her eyes and said, "Zoe, I don't want you messing this up, trying to make some big deal. Let's just get the book published."

Zoe waved her hand and said, "Relax. I've got it all under control. Put your headphones back on and listen to your agent go to work."

Natalie pulled on the headphones, and Zoe sat down, turned on her phone, and dialed Hannah Nelson's number. She answered right away, and Natalie thought, *Poor woman, she's working through her lunchtime again.*

Natalie could hear only Zoe's half of the conversation.

"Hannah? This is Zee Zee Reisman from the Sherry Clutch Agency, and I'm returning your call. I am so glad you like Cassandra's book. I think you're very smart to pick up on it right away. . . . Yes, yes, I can understand that . . . but still, if you're asking me to stop sending the book to other publishers, then you must have a very strong interest. . . . Uh-huh, yes—of course. . . . I understand. So, Hannah, what is the next step here? . . . Yes, that sounds good. . . . Sure, but Wednesday would be better. I don't want to let this cool off. . . . Fine. . . . Yes, I understand. . . . This is good, and I'll talk to you on

Wednesday. . . . And thank you. Good-bye, now."

Natalie yanked off the headphones and stood up to look over the top of the partition. "Well?" she said. "Does she want to publish it?"

Zoe nodded. "I can tell she does, but she says she has to talk to the rest of the editorial committee. She's trying to sound like she's not excited about it, but when I asked her to call me Wednesday instead of Thursday, she said yes right away. I think she really wants this book!"

Five minutes after her first conversation with Zee Zee Reisman, Hannah Nelson knocked lightly on Letha Springfield's open door and stuck her head inside the office. Letha was on the phone, but she motioned for Hannah to come in and sit down. Letha's office was four times the size of Hannah's, complete with a couch and a little round conference table next to windows that looked down into a plaza with trees and a fountain. Hannah sat at the table and tried to look like she wasn't listening.

When Letha hung up the phone, she said, "So, did you talk to the agent?"

Hannah said, "Yes, and she said she'd like to hear back from us on Wednesday. So could you look this over and see if you agree with me? I really think this is a good one, and if we can come to terms quickly, this book could even make it into the summer catalog."

Letha's eyebrows went up and she pursed her lips. "So you really think this book is worth the rush?"

Hannah paused. Talking with Letha was dangerous. She enjoyed making her people take a strong position on everything. That way, if there were problems later on, it was never her fault. But Hannah felt sure about this book, so she said, "Definitely—and I'll put in the extra hours to get it done right."

Letha stood up, and so did Hannah. Letha said, "Fine. I'll read it tonight, and we'll talk about it tomorrow. And I'm glad I had you read it over the weekend."

Hannah handed her the envelope with the manuscript. "Thanks, Letha."

On the bus Monday afternoon Natalie didn't want to talk about the book. She was afraid she might jinx it or say something stupid and give away her secret. But just before they got to the terminal in Hoboken, her mom brought it up.

"You know that new book I told you about last night?" she said.

Natalie gulped and nodded. "Yeah?"

"Well, I talked to the agent today, and Letha's reading it tonight. I'm really excited about it."

Natalie couldn't resist. She said, "So, what do you know about the author?"

Her mom shrugged. "Nothing, really. Except that she's a good writer. And she has a good ear for the way kids talk, and she knows how to keep a story moving forward." Her mom paused and looked out the window. Then she said, "I think finding a new writer is even more fun than working with someone who's already great. It's like . . . it's like finding a new island out in the middle of the ocean. And once you find it, from then on that island goes on every new map. Then every time you look at a map, you see the island, and you say to yourself, 'That's the one I found!'"

"That's neat, Mom." It was quiet for a minute or so, and then Natalie said, "You really like being an editor, don't you?"

"Yes, I do." Hannah turned to smile at Natalie. "There's only one thing I like better— and that's being your mom."

Natalie smiled back, and the bus pulled into the station.

CHAPTER 16

Poker, Anyone?

Right in the middle of Wednesday's morning meeting Zoe's beeper started jiggling. She nudged Natalie, pulled her sweater up, and pointed at it. Natalie craned her neck to read the number and then frowned.

In the hall on the way to science Natalie said, "I don't get it. I can tell the call is from Shipley, because all the numbers there start with 555. But it's not my mom's number."

"Maybe she called from a meeting in a different room," suggested Zoe. "But anyway, we know her number, so I'll just call her at lunchtime like we did Monday."

When Zee Zee called Hannah Nelson from

her soundproof office in the Deary School library, Natalie listened. Right away she could tell there was something wrong.

"Hannah? This is Zee Zee from the Sherry Clutch Agency. What's the news? . . . Oh. . . . I see. Well, I'm sorry about that. . . . All right. Good-bye."

Natalie tore off the headphones and stood up. "They're saying no? But she liked it so much! I don't get it."

Zoe shook her head. "No, that's not it. The good news is that they like the book, and they definitely want it . . . but your mom said someone else is going to be the editor. She didn't sound very happy about it. It's someone named Letha Springfield."

The color drained from Natalie's face, and she sat down with a *thump*. Zoe stood up and looked at her. "Are you all right?"

Natalie said, "Letha—she's my mom's boss, the one I'm always telling you about. She *can't* be the editor. She's awful! And she doesn't even like kids. Whenever she sees me, it's like she wants to push me into a closet or something. I really want my mom to be the editor.

Can't we do something?"

Zoe said, "I'm not sure."

After school Ms. Clayton listened while the girls told her the good news and then the bad news.

Natalie said, "I'm not kidding. I do *not* want that lady to be the editor. There must be *something* we can do."

Ms. Clayton looked out the window a few moments and then said, "Well . . . there is something you could try . . . but it might upset the whole deal. It all depends on how much they want your book."

Natalie frowned, "I don't care. I'll try anything."

Ms. Clayton turned to Zoe and said, "You're going to have to be a pretty tough agent if this is going to work. Do you think you're ready to play some poker?"

"Poker?" said Zoe. "I *love* poker. I beat my dad and my sisters at it all the time."

Ms. Clayton smiled wryly, looking from Zoe to Natalie, and said, "Why am I not surprised?"

Natalie frowned. "But this time you're not

playing for matchsticks, Zoe."

"No problem," Zoe said.

And Natalie thought, *Yeah, that's what the captain of the* Titanic *said.*

Even after Ms. Clayton had explained her idea, Natalie still felt like she was on a sinking ship.

Hannah Nelson hurried to Letha's office at three o'clock on Wednesday afternoon. Letha was pacing behind her desk, her high heels clicking as she crossed and recrossed the hard plastic chair mat.

Hannah said, "What's up?"

Letha stopped, face toward the windows, her back to Hannah. Turning around, she grabbed the high back of her gray leather desk chair, her fingernails digging into the padding. "The *nerve* of that woman! Talking to me that way . . . giving me an *ultimatum*! Unbelievable! Tell me—did you make some sort of promise to her? Think very, *very* carefully before you answer me."

Hannah was confused. "Promise? To whom?"

"To that *woman*!" stormed Letha. "Zee Zee, the agent from the loony bin, that's who! What did you tell her about that manuscript?"

Hannah gulped. Letha was never a picnic to work for, but when she was like this, things got broken, things like vases and computers—and careers. "I . . . I didn't say anything out of the ordinary. I told her the manuscript had promise, and that we wanted to think about it—and I asked her not to send it anywhere else until we got back to her today."

"And that's all?" There was a threat in Letha's voice, lurking below the shrill surface.

Hannah met Letha's glare without blinking. "Yes," she said evenly. "I'm certain I said nothing more."

Momentarily satisfied, Letha wheeled away, setting her chair spinning. "Then what we're dealing with is crazy people, both her and her writer! Because Zee Zee says that Cassandra Day has fixed on the idea that no one but *you* can edit her book!"

Hannah hid her feelings and asked, "And what did you tell her?"

"Tell her?" raged Letha. "Tell her? I told her things don't work that way in the real world, and that she'd better go and shake her author by the shoulders and get her to wake up. I told her that *I'm* the editor in chief at Shipley Junior Books, and that I like this manuscript enough to take it on and edit it myself, and that if her little Miss Day doesn't care for that, then she could take her manuscript and throw it off the Empire State Building! *That's* what I told her!"

Hannah wished she could leave, but she nodded slowly and said, "Oh . . . I see. . . ."

Letha wasn't done. "And do you know what she said to me? She said, 'Well, Ms. Springfield, I *always* try to do all I can for my writers, so perhaps we both had better think about this—as if *I'm* suddenly going to change my mind! The *nerve* of that woman!"

There was a moment of quiet, and Hannah asked, "So, what are you going to do?"

Letha planted both feet and crossed her arms. "Unless I get an apology, we will not publish that book." Then, pointing with one long index finger, Letha added, "And if you have *any* contact with that agent, I want to hear about it, is that clear?"

Hannah nodded. "Certainly."

Letha sat in her chair and spun away to look out the window. The meeting was over.

Hannah got out quickly, glad that she still had her job. Letha's door had been open, and everyone on the floor must have heard her shouting. She was glad Natalie wasn't around. Natalie had called right after school to say she'd be waiting for her in the lobby at five.

Hannah was suddenly desperate for a candy bar, so she walked to the elevator and headed toward the employee snack room on the fifteenth floor. Four minutes and one Hershey bar later Hannah sat alone at a small, round table feeling sorry for herself. She would have loved to edit that book. And she felt sorry for the author. It was a bad break. This could delay the publication of the book for at least six months, maybe more—maybe forever. And it was such a good book. It would be a gain for some other publishing house, and a loss for Shipley.

But most of all Hannah felt sorry for Zee Zee. Hannah was puzzled. Zee Zee had seemed so smart, so capable—but now it appeared very likely that Zee Zee was about to get run over by a steamroller. Hannah had thought that everybody in the New York publishing world knew about Letha Springfield. Letha was the wrong person to have for an enemy. And by the time someone figured that out, it was usually too late.

Natalie knew why her mom was so silent and tense on the cab ride to the Port Authority Bus Terminal Wednesday evening. Once they'd boarded and the bus was heading down the ramp toward the Lincoln Tunnel, Hannah Nelson settled back in her seat and let out a deep sigh.

Natalie said, "Another one of those long meetings today, Mom?"

With a grim smile her mom said, "No, actually it was two short ones, both with Letha."

"Oh?"

"Yup—one first thing in the morning, and then another one in the afternoon. They were both about that manuscript, 'The Cheater.'"

"What—didn't she like it?"

Her mom let out a bitter little laugh. "That's not the problem. She liked it a lot—you'd have to be a moron not to. But first thing in the morning she calls me in and says, 'This is a terrific book. This writer really knows kids, don't you think? You can just feel the zits popping out on their faces. Thanks for spotting it. I'm going to handle it myself.'" Hannah turned to look out the window.

Natalie said, "Can she do that, like, just take it away?"

Turning back to Natalie, her mom said, "Letha? Letha can do pretty much whatever she wants to. What's so upsetting is she does this all the time. I find a good property, and then she takes it over and steals all the glory, if you can call it that. It's not the glory I want. It's just that I'm trying to build a career here, and Letha's already got a great one. And this book, well, it has real promise, especially since it's a first novel. This is what an editor like me hopes for—a new writer with a strong first book who has the promise of developing into something more. That's how an editor gets noticed in this business. I just happen to be cursed with a selfish boss, and there's not much I can do about it."

"What about the second meeting?" asked Natalie.

"At about three she yells for me to come to her office, and then she rants and raves about this agent—her name is Zee Zee—because she called Letha and said that the author wants *me* to be the editor for her book. So Letha practically accuses me of going behind her back and making promises to the agent—which I would never do. So now Letha's got her high heels dug in, and she's saying if it doesn't happen her way, then it doesn't happen. So the book is probably not going to get published, at least not at our company." Hannah paused and then said, "What I don't get is, why would the author be so determined to have me be her editor, anyway?"

Natalie said, "It's because you're a great editor, that's why. And the author probably heard about you, and the agent could probably tell just from talking with you that you're nice, too—not like that witch Letha. Don't you just *hate* her?"

"No, I don't hate her. . . . I just don't understand her, that's all. It seems like it would be so easy for her to ease up a little. She's got all this talent, she looks great, she makes good money, and she really is an amazing editor. I guess she just has some other issues that make her feel like she has to keep grabbing more and more for herself. In a way I feel sorry for her." She almost added "And I feel even sorrier for myself," but she didn't.

Hannah fell silent and turned to look out the window again.

Natalie was quiet too. She wished she could comfort her mom. She'd say, "Don't worry, Mom. Because if Ms. Clayton and Zoe know how to play poker half as well as they think they do, then help is on the way."

CHAPTER 17

High Stakes, Aces wild

When a package arrived by messenger at nine fifteen on Thursday morning, Kelley Collins double-checked the address label.

Kelley had been Tom Morton's secretary for the past six years as he worked his way up through the ranks at Shipley Publishing Company. Whenever he had jumped a rung on the ladder, Kelley had jumped with him. And now Tom was the president and publisher of Shipley Junior Books, and Kelley was his Executive Assistant.

Mr. Morton didn't usually get packages from agents, but this one was clearly addressed to him, so Kelley opened it. He wouldn't be in the office until one o'clock today, so she had plenty of time to get his correspondence and his afternoon appointments organized.

She started to read the cover letter from the agent, and when she got to the name Letha Springfield, she stiffened. Her eyes narrowed and her mouth formed an involuntary frown. Kelley had been watching Letha Springfield carefully for the past two years. Every time Letha and the other editors in chief came to a meeting on the sixteenth floor, Kelley had the feeling that Letha was measuring the windows in Tom Morton's office for curtains—*her* curtains.

Kelley finished reading the letter and then looked at the manuscript. *Good title*, she thought. Kelley flipped the title page over and began reading. After three pages she was hooked. She read the story off and on all morning and then finished it over the noon hour. And when she got back from lunch, Kelley put the letter and the manuscript at the top of the stack in Mr. Morton's in box.

At one fifteen on Thursday afternoon Tom Morton called to Kelley through his open door.

"Kelley, would you take this down to fourteen and give it to Letha? She really ought to handle this herself." When Kelley walked in, he was holding out the manuscript and the letter from the agent.

Kelley took the manuscript from him, and Tom looked down at the next item on his desk. But Kelley didn't leave, and when he noticed, Tom looked up again and said, "Something else?"

Kelley shifted her weight from one foot to the other, then plunged in. Holding up the letter, she said, "Mr. Morton, I know this situation is sort of a can of worms, but did you look at the story? It's a great book—I read the whole thing . . . over my lunch hour. I think it might be worth taking a look at . . . if you don't mind my saying so."

Tom Morton never minded Kelley saying what was on her mind. She had kept him from making at least a dozen mistakes over the years—several mistakes that could have delayed his promotions, and one or two that could have cost him his job. She had the instincts of a mother lion, and Tom was glad to have her looking out for him.

With a smile he pushed the papers on his desk to one side, took the manuscript back from her, and began reading. Kelley turned and left his office, pulling the door shut behind her.

Ten minutes later Tom Morton buzzed Kelley on the speakerphone.

"Yes, Mr. Morton?"

"Kelley, hold my phone calls for an hour or so, would you? I'd like to finish reading this manuscript."

Kelley Collins smiled at her phone and said, "Will do."

At precisely 3:46 on Thursday afternoon Letha Springfield and Hannah Nelson each received an E-mail message, and the little mail-delivery chime bonged on both of their computers. Letha ignored the chime because she was on the phone, but Hannah clicked on her E-mail icon and read the message right away.

tmorton@shipleybooks.com/ed/smpt//inhouse/
3:45 PM ***2.19.00
From: Tom Morton
To: Letha Springfield

Cc:

Bcc: Hannah Nelson

Re: The Cheater manuscript

Letha—

It's odd for an agent to send anything directly to me these days, so I took note when someone named Zee Zee Reisman messengered me a manuscript this morning. It's called The Cheater, and from the cover letter, I gather you've seen it too.

I started reading it—couldn't stop. Made me remember all those years I spent as an editor. I hate to step in, but it's clear that unless we put Hannah on this project, we'll lose the book, and frankly we can't afford to. I smell a hit here, and if we have to let a headstrong author have her own way in order to keep the book, then I say we let her.

I've called Susan Yau in marketing and asked her to save a half page for this in the summer catalog. I know a June pub date is pushing it, but this one could build nicely and be strong right into the fall.

Have Hannah handle the deal and the editing, and I'd like her to keep me in the loop on this. Susan will call her in a day or so for catalog information.

Thanks,

Tom

As Hannah read the E-mail, her throat tightened up. Her heart raced and she felt as if she couldn't breathe. Hannah knew this feeling. It was fear.

Looking at the heading of the E-mail again, she saw that her copy was a "bcc"—a blind copy. That meant Tom Morton had sent Hannah a copy of his message to Letha, but Letha didn't know about the copy.

Hannah took several deep breaths to try to clear her head. She thought, *Doesn't Tom know what an impossible situation this puts me in? Doesn't he know it's already hard enough to work for Letha?*

Nervously Hannah jumped up from her chair. Standing on her tiptoes in her doorway, she peeked over the top of the cubicle dividers to look across at Letha's office. Letha was there, talking on the phone, smiling and nodding. Hannah thought, *She must not have read it yet.*

Hannah sat down again and looked at the E-mail still open on her computer screen. She tried to think calmly, but she couldn't. The message was like a time bomb in Letha's computer, ticking away. Any minute now Letha would click it open and—*boom!*

Hannah shook her head. She had to admire this Zee Zee Reisman. Sending the manuscript directly to Tom Morton was a gutsy thing to do. She thought, *This woman is incredibly brave— or else she's incredibly stupid.*

"Hi."

Hannah almost jumped out of her shoes. She wheeled around. "Oh! . . . It's you, Natalie! Ooohhph—you surprised me." Instantly Hannah turned around and grabbed her purse from the bottom drawer of her desk. She pulled out two dollars and said, "I think you'd better go up to the lunchroom and study this afternoon, honey. Here's some snack money."

Natalie looked at her mom. She said, "Are you okay, Mom? You look . . . you look kind of . . . funny."

Hannah laughed nervously. "Just a lot going on today, that's all. Now, you run along—and stay put. I'll come up there and get you on my way out, okay?"

"Sure, Mom. See you later."

• • • • •

Letha Springfield stomped off the elevator onto the sixteenth floor. It was six minutes after four o'clock. Five minutes earlier Letha had read her E-mail from Tom Morton.

Grim, unsmiling, Letha didn't slow down. She glared at the receptionist, who scrambled to push the security button just as Letha reached the door to the executive offices.

Striding on, Letha approached Tom Morton's office. She had a piece of paper in her hand. As she went marching right past Kelley Collins into Tom Morton's office, she waved it and said, "Mr. Morton is *expecting* me!" The office door slammed shut behind her.

Kelley kept tapping away at her keyboard. A nearly invisible smile tickled the corners of her mouth. She wished she could be a fly on the wall in her boss's office.

At four forty-five Hannah was working on a letter to one of her authors. She heard a rustle of papers behind her. The hairs on the back of her neck stood up. Hannah tensed and then turned her chair to face the doorway. It was Letha.

"Here." Letha's voice sounded like a shovel plunging into a pile of gravel. She handed Hannah a manuscript. Hannah didn't have to look to know what it was, but she did. Then she did her best to look surprised. Letha said, "I've decided you should handle this one. After all, we don't want our sensitive little Miss Author to get her tummy all tied up in knots, now do we? So I want you to take it from here."

Hannah tried to keep the right mixture of surprise, confusion, and obedient acceptance in her voice and gestures. She said, "But . . . well . . . I'll be glad to. Are you sure you want me to?"

Coldly, evenly, Letha said, "Very sure." And with that, she turned and walked briskly back toward her office.

Hannah took three or four deep breaths. She thought, *If I ever get fired from here, I'll go train tigers for Ringling Brothers—it'll feel like a vacation!*

When her mom came to get her in the snack room, Natalie thought her mom's face looked strange. She seemed to be in a big hurry, too. She was silent in the elevator, and once on the ground floor, she took Natalie's hand and practically dragged her across the lobby and then squeezed into the same compartment of the revolving door with her. Once they were out of the building and down the block near where they caught their cab, her mom started to laugh and swing Natalie's arm back and forth, almost giddy.

Natalie said, "What's all this about?"

Hannah stopped to catch her breath and at the same time held up her hand to flag a vacant cab. Then she giggled and said, "You'll never *believe* what happened at work today!"

But her mom was wrong. Natalie believed every word of it.

CHAPTER 18

The Long Arm of the Law

Ms. Clayton sat at a small, round table in the Linden Room with Natalie and Zoe on a Thursday afternoon. It had been just a week since they sent Tom Morton a copy of Natalie's manuscript, but with Hannah Nelson handling the project, there had been rapid progress.

Hannah had found Zee Zee Reisman to be a very cooperative agent. When Hannah offered a royalty advance of six thousand dollars, Zee Zee accepted right away—not a single counteroffer. Hannah could have paid as much as ten thousand dollars for the book—she had authorization from Tom Morton himself. Zee Zee, on the other hand, had been told by

Natalie to take the first offer with absolutely no negotiating. Accepting that offer without arguing was one of the hardest things Zoe had ever done.

Thanks to Hannah's efficiency and Zee Zee's cooperation, the entire membership of the Deary School Publishing Club was now staring at a stack of paper on the little, round table. It was the contract, all fourteen pages of it, in triplicate. By signing the contract, Cassandra Day ("hereinafter referred to as THE AUTHOR") would grant permission to Shipley Junior Books ("hereinafter referred to as THE PUBLISHER") to publish *The Cheater* ("hereinafter referred to as THE WORK") for "the full duration of copyright"—which meant all of Cassandra's life plus another fifty years after she died.

At the end of the fourteen pages there was a place for Zee Zee Reisman ("hereinafter referred to as THE AGENT") to sign, and there was a place for Cassandra Day to sign. Cassandra Day also had to write her Social Security number on the contract. All three copies had to be signed and dated and returned to Shipley Junior Books as soon as possible.

Patting the stack of paper, Ms. Clayton spoke first. "I know I'm supposed to be your adviser, but I really don't know what to tell you. This contract is a legally binding document. I'm pretty sure you have to be at least eighteen years old to sign a contract yourself, maybe even twenty-one—and I know you should completely understand all the words before you ever sign anything."

Zoe had been enjoying her role as the bigshot agent, the queen of the problem solvers. With a little toss of her head she said, "I know all about contracts. You write down the deal, then you sign it, and then you do what you said you would. My dad says that's all there is to it."

Natalie gave Zoe a sideways look. "If that's all there is to it, Zoe, then every cab driver in New York City would become a lawyer."

Zoe made a face at Natalie and then said, "So, what do you think we should do, Ms. Clayton?"

Looking from Zoe to Natalie, she said, "I don't think we have any choice, girls. We need to talk to a lawyer."

Natalie nodded, and glancing at Zoe, she said, "I agree—a *real* lawyer. I think we should talk to Zoe's dad."

"No way," said Zoe. "No parents, remember?"

"But remember what you said to me about my mom? It's the same kind of thing. He's not just your dad, Zoe. He's your *lawyer*."

"But what if he says he has to tell your mom about everything?" said Zoe. "He might feel like he really has to."

"Not if I tell him he can't," said Natalie. "If you tell something to a lawyer, he's not allowed to tell anyone else, right, Ms. Clayton?"

Ms. Clayton nodded. "That's true. So what do you think, Zoe?"

Zoe shrugged and said, "Well, I guess it'll be all right. I know my dad can figure out what we should do . . . and he probably won't charge us anything either."

At noon on Friday, Natalie called her mom. She asked if she could ride home with Zoe after school. Her mom said, "That'll be fine. How about I pick you up at her house at six o'clock. We'll get some food in the city—and maybe I'll call your uncle and see if he wants to see a movie with us."

So it was all settled. Except Natalie and Zoe weren't going to Zoe's house after school—at least not right away. First they had to have a talk with their lawyer.

Zoe and Natalie walked into the reception area of Crouch, Pruitt, and Reisman at three fifteen. Zoe had been to her dad's office only once or twice on a weekday, and that was a long time ago. The receptionist didn't recognize her.

The tall young woman put her hand over the mouthpiece of the telephone headset looped over her right ear. She smiled and said, "May I help you?"

Zoe said, "We're here to see Robert Reisman."

The receptionist's smile dimmed, and she said, "I see. Do you have an appointment?"

Zoe said, "No, but I know he's here." Zoe had called her dad's secretary from school at noon to make sure about that.

The receptionist frowned slightly and raised one eyebrow. "And who may I say is here to see him?"

Zoe smiled sweetly and said, "Tell him it's his favorite daughter, Zoe."

Three minutes later a surprised Robert Reisman was sitting in a chair across from Zoe and Natalie. Zoe had settled back into the cushions of the couch, but Natalie sat on the front edge.

Looking from face to face, he said, "So, what's going on here? I mean, I'm happy to see you, Zoe, and you, too, Natalie . . . but let's hear what's on your mind—unless this is a purely social visit."

As planned, Natalie spoke first. Opening her backpack, she took out the contract and handed it across the coffee table to Zoe's dad. "No, this is a business visit, Mr. Reisman. I need to have a lawyer look at this contract."

Zoe's dad was already doing that, peering down through his reading glasses, flipping from page to page. Nodding his head, he said, "This is a publishing contract—looks pretty standard. What's this got to do with—" He stopped in midsentence, his eyes fixed on the last page. Looking up quickly at Zoe, he said, "'Zee Zee Reisman, agent for THE AUTHOR'? Is this a coincidence? This is a project for a class, and you want me to look at it, right? Is that it?"

Zoe smiled a knowing little smile at her dad and nodded toward Natalie, as if to say, "Ask her." On cue, Natalie said, "No, it's a real contract. I wrote a book, and my pen name is Cassandra Day. And Zoe—that is, Zee Zee—she's been my agent."

Robert Reisman sat back in his chair and looked at his daughter. "No kidding?"

Zoe said, "No kidding. We wanted to get Natalie's book published, and we're *this* close, but our adviser at school said we needed to talk to a lawyer to see if we could even sign this contract."

Leaning forward again, Mr. Reisman said, "Your *adviser*? At school?"

Natalie nodded. "Ms. Clayton. She's our English teacher. She helped us rent the office where we get mail and phone calls."

"You have . . . you have an *office*?" Robert Reisman looked from girl to girl as they both nodded yes.

Natalie ignored the lawyer's amazement and quickly described the steps that had led to the

Shipley Junior Books
2000 Avenue of the Americas
New York, NY 10000

CONTRACT

AGREEMENT, entered into between SHIPLEY JUNIOR
BOOKS (hereinafter referred to as THE PUBLISHER) and
CASSANDRA DAY (hereinafter referred to as THE AUTHOR).

In consideration of the premises hereinafter set forth, Publisher
and Author hereby agree with respect to the work tentatively
entitled

THE CHEATER
(hereinafter referred to as THE WORK)

contract. Then she said, "So what we need to know is, can we sign this contract and have it be . . . you know, legal?"

"Legal?" Mr. Reisman was at a loss for words, something that did not happen to him very often. Making a visible effort to think like a lawyer, he said, "Well, you are both underage—but you have in fact already delivered the manuscript to the publisher, correct?"

Natalie nodded.

The lawyer went on, "And it could be argued that concealment of the author's age was not an effort to commit fraud but was merely part of the same principle leading her to use a pseudonym in order to have her work taken seriously—is that a fair statement of the facts?"

Natalie nodded again, expecting that any moment he would ask her to put her hand on the Bible and swear to tell the truth, the whole truth, and nothing but the truth.

"And at any time did any person at the publishing company indicate that the age of either the agent or the author might affect whether or not the work was acceptable or this contract could be issued?"

Each girl shook her head no to that.

"And did anyone ever ask you your age, or did either of you ever volunteer false information about your age to anyone at the publishing company?"

Again, each girl shook her head no.

"Then I think that each of you should be able to sign this contract and have it be legally binding—provided, of course, that you each have a parent sign an affidavit that says you are entering into the agreement with their full knowledge and consent." He winked at Zoe and said, "I think I can find someone to vouch for Zee Zee."

Natalie looked at Zoe and then back to Mr. Reisman. Natalie said, "But that's a problem for me. You see, my mom? . . . Well, she works at Shipley Junior Books. She's an editor . . . and she's the editor for this book. So I can't really have her sign that . . . whatever you called it, saying it's okay. I mean, I'm sure it would be fine with her, but I don't want to let her know it's me until the book is all edited. And my dad, well, you know about my dad."

Robert Reisman sat back in his chair again

and rubbed his chin. "Hmm. Yes, I can see the problem. You don't feel free to get your mom's prior consent because if she knew, she could be accused of giving you special treatment—it's called a conflict-of-interest situation. Hmm . . ." And the lawyer paused again. Then he asked, "How about a grandparent, or some near relative we could inform of the situation? That way, if this matter ever came before a judge, we could show that we wanted to make sure you had guidance from an adult who had your best interest in mind. Anyone who fits that description?"

Instantly Natalie said, "Uncle Fred! He's my dad's brother. He lives here in the city, and he's the one who helped us with everything after my dad died, and sometimes we go on trips with him in the summer, and he comes to our house all the time, and we go to his—he's a close relative, right?"

Zoe's dad asked, "Do you know his phone number?"

Natalie said, "No, but I know his address, and I know he runs an advertising company called Nelson Creative."

Mr. Reisman handed Natalie a pad of yellow paper and a pen, and she wrote down Frederick T. Nelson's address.

Three minutes later Natalie was talking to her uncle at his office through the speakerphone on Mr. Reisman's desk. "Uncle Fred? It's me, Natalie."

"Natalie? This is a surprise! Is everything all right? Your voice sounds funny."

"That's because I'm using a speakerphone. Everything's fine, but I need to ask you something. I'm calling you from the office of my friend Zoe's dad. He's a lawyer, and he's helping me with . . . a problem."

Natalie took about five minutes to tell her uncle what was happening, and Zoe chimed in whenever she thought Natalie left something out. Then Natalie introduced Mr. Reisman, and he and Uncle Fred talked about the details. When he'd explained the legal situation, Mr. Reisman said, "I've looked over the contract, and it's a fairly standard publishing agreement—which means it heavily favors the publisher. Still, if you can sign an affidavit that states you and Natalie understand what's going on, and that until her mom can be informed, you are acting as next-of-kin adviser, then I see no reason why my daughter and your niece can't sign the contract and move ahead with this."

Fred Nelson said, "Well, if you think it's all right for your daughter, then I guess it should be fine for Natalie. If you send me the affidavit, I'll sign it and get it notarized and get it back to you right away." Then Uncle Fred said, "Natalie?"

"Yes?"

"Way to go, kid. Sounds like a great book, and I can't wait to talk to your mom after she finds out it's yours. And another thing—tell your agent there that whenever she's ready, I've got a job waiting for her here at Nelson Creative."

Zoe had been slumped on the couch, feeling a little neglected. She perked up and said, "Thanks, Mr. Nelson."

Grinning across his desk at Zoe, Mr. Reisman said, "Sorry, Fred, but Zoe's already an honorary partner right here at Crouch, Pruitt, and Reisman."

Then Natalie said, "Hey! I want everyone to remember that first of all she's *my* agent!"

Uncle Fred said, "Well, hang on to her, Natalie—she's pure gold."

Natalie beamed at Zoe and said, "I know, Uncle Fred . . . I know."

The buzz of the intercom startled Ms. Clayton as she sat at her desk marking some eighth-grade essays.

It was Mrs. Fratchi. The school secretary didn't like teachers getting phone calls at school, and when Mrs. Fratchi disapproved of something, she never tried to hide it. "Miss Clayton? There's a *personal* telephone call for you on line two in the teachers' room."

Ms. Clayton said, "Thank you," but Mrs. Fratchi had already clicked off the intercom.

Thinking it must be Natalie, Ms. Clayton hurried down the hall and into the empty lounge. She picked up the handset and punched the blinking button. "Hello?"

A woman's voice said, "Ms. Clayton?"

"Yes . . ."

"Please hold a moment."

Then a clear, strong voice said, "Ms. Clayton, this is Robert Reisman. I'm Zoe's father."

"H-hello, Mr. Reisman." She gulped, and her heart started pounding. "Did . . . did the girls come and . . . and talk to you?"

"Yup—just left. Tell me about this office, Ms. Clayton."

Laura Clayton couldn't tell much from his voice. He didn't sound mad, but it wasn't really a friendly tone either. She gulped again and said, "Well, it's one of those instant office places on upper Broadway. It's near where I live, so I stop in to pick up the mail. And they have a beeper service so that we . . . I mean, so that Zoe can return phone calls."

"Zoe talked on the phone with these people?"

"Well, yes," said Ms. Clayton, "but . . . but not a lot. Just when she had to."

"How about the rent on this office, Ms. Clayton?"

"I . . . I was going to explain that to you. When Zoe got the idea to rent the office—"

Mr. Reisman broke in, "Renting the office was Zoe's idea?"

"Oh, yes. I . . . I was just her . . . well, her helper."

"Okay," he said, "go on."

"Well, Zoe brought me an envelope of money."

"How much money?"

Ms. Clayton winced and said, "Well . . . it was five hundred dollars."

"Did you say five *hundred*?"

"Yes, five hundred dollars."

"In cash?"

"Yes, all in cash." Laura Clayton did not feel this conversation was going well.

Robert Reisman was silent, so Ms. Clayton continued. "Zoe said it was her money, and I didn't doubt it, but . . . but I didn't want to spend that money without . . . well, without permission. So I paid for the office with my own credit card."

"And what about the cash?"

"I . . . I opened a new savings account at my bank. It's all there."

The lawyer was quiet for a few moments. Then

he said, "Ms. Clayton, I'm going to say something, and I hope you are listening very carefully."

Ms. Clayton was having a hard time hearing anything except the thumping of her runaway heartbeat. Weakly she said, "Yes?"

Robert Reisman continued, "Ms. Clayton, I don't know if helping the girls to do all this was wise on your part. However, I do know this. You have been very courageous, and I can't thank you enough. I wish you could have been here to listen to these two kids tell me about this deal. This is real learning here, you know what I mean? Real stuff in the real world? I can tell you one thing—I will never again groan when I pay Zoe's tuition bill. If it helps to pay your salary, Ms. Clayton, then it is money well spent."

Ms. Clayton was stunned, and a silly grin crept over her face. She managed to say, "Thank you, sir."

"And Ms. Clayton, send me a bill for that rent right away, here at my office. Zoe'll give you the address, all right?"

"Yes . . . yes, of course, Mr. Reisman."

"Don't take this the wrong way, Ms.

Clayton, but I hope you stay a teacher for a long, long time. Kids need teachers who aren't afraid of life, don't you think?"

"Yes . . . yes, and thank you."

"No, Ms. Clayton," said the lawyer, "thank *you*!"

Cassandra Day
% The Shevy Clotch Literary
723 West 93rd Agency
NYC 10023

CHAPTER 19

The Red Pencil Blues

Six days after the contract had been signed and returned to Shipley Junior Books, Ms. Clayton stopped at Offices Unlimited on her way home. Today the office manager handed her a large brown envelope addressed to Cassandra Day, care of the Sherry Clutch Literary Agency.

In English class the next afternoon Ms. Clayton passed a note to Natalie and Zoe asking them to come to a meeting.

When they were sitting at the small, round table after school, Natalie opened the envelope. It was a five-page letter from her editor, along with a copy of her story. The manuscript was littered with dozens of Post-it notes—the yellow ones were editorial suggestions, and the pink ones flagged grammar questions. It looked like Hannah Nelson had worn out at least three red pencils.

The letter began, "Dear Cassandra: Thank you for this wonderful first draft. Now that your contract is all squared away, we can get down to work."

Natalie's heart sank. She thumbed through the manuscript, flipping from note to note. "Look at all these—this is going take forever! I thought the book was done, and I thought it was good, too. And . . . look."

Ms. Clayton took the letter from Natalie. As she read through the first two pages the teacher began to nod and smile. She was impressed. She said, "So now we know what real editors do. This is a wonderful letter, Natalie. She's telling you how to make a good book into a great book, that's all. Your mom really knows what she's doing."

Natalie said, "Yeah, she knows what *she's* doing, but what about me?"

Zoe wasn't sympathetic. "Quit whining, Natalie. You wanted to be an author, and now you are one. So your editor gives you a bunch of good ideas to make the book better—so what? You're an author now, so you have to do the work."

"Well, you're a big help, Miss Know-it-all!" snapped Natalie.

"Girls!" said Ms. Clayton. "We don't need any sarcasm—and we don't need criticism, either." Then in a gentler tone she said, "Natalie, just take this home this weekend and see how it goes—maybe spend only half an hour on it. It doesn't all have to be done at once. If you get stuck, well, that's why you have an editor. It's her job to help you do your best work."

Natalie and Zoe went down the front steps of the school. Ms. Clayton had sent them on their way together, but neither had said a word on the walk through the halls.

Natalie got to the bottom of the steps and turned left as if she was just going to walk to her bus, but Zoe took her by the arm.

"Wait, Natalie." Natalie stopped and turned to face her. Zoe said, "Listen . . . I'm sorry I called you a whiner. It's just that . . . well, I feel like my part in all this is over, and I . . . and I don't know what to do."

"So how do you think *I* feel?" snapped Natalie. "I wish we hadn't started this. I mean, my mom almost got fired, and she still could, for all I know. And now I've got all this extra work to do, and I'm still not sure the book is going to turn out right. And then it gets published, and then what if the book reviewers hate it and no one buys it—then what?"

Zoe looked into Natalie's eyes. The fear and the worry was so intense it made Natalie look feverish. Instantly Zoe was furious with herself for being so stupid . . . so . . . so selfish.

"Then what?" asked Zoe. "If some reviewer doesn't like it? So what? It just means he's an idiot. How could anyone *not* like this book, Natalie? This book is so good that even Lethal Letha the Grumphead liked it, remember? And all those little changes your mom—I mean, your *editor* wants you to make? I know you can figure them out. You're good at this. And your book? It's only gonna get better and better, honest."

Natalie smiled a little and said, "Do you think so?"

Zoe nodded and said, "I *know* so!"

Already Zoe could see Natalie's eyes changing. She could see her smart, talented, confident friend coming back to life. And with a surge of fierce joy Zoe could see that her part in all this *wasn't* over, not by a long shot.

Natalie discovered that the editing process wasn't glamorous, and it wasn't a lot of fun, but at least it was creative. It was work—slow, steady work. It was a careful look at every word, every sentence, paragraph, and chapter. It was a methodical tracing of each character, each story-line, each rise and fall of the action, each of the points along the path that led to the end of the book. And always, everything had to be judged to see if it supported the overall theme and the deeper ideas that made her book more than just a story.

During four weeks of revisions the book got steadily better. Every day, and especially during their bus rides home, Natalie was tempted to ask her mom about the book she was editing. But she didn't. Natalie felt like that would have been unfair . . . like cheating.

She also learned that the editing process was when an author and an editor got to know each other. When one said, "Let's cut this out of the book," and the other said, "No, I really think it should stay," each learned something new about the other. It was like a very long conversation about . . . about life. Natalie felt she was getting to know her mom in a way she never had before. When a note from her mom asked Cassandra Day, "Does Sean really have to seem so mean at this part of the story?"—Natalie could hear her mom and dad telling her how important it was to be kind.

And when Cassandra Day wrote back and said, "Sean's not really being mean here, it's just that his feelings are hurt, and the narrator hasn't figured it out yet," Hannah read the note and smiled, and suggested a way to make that clearer to the reader without giving too much away too soon.

And during the editing process the author and the editor came to respect each other's ideas and insights more and more.

Near the end of the manuscript there was a note from the editor about Angela's father. Of all the notes, it was the one that meant the most to Natalie.

Cassandra—

There are only a few small changes I'd suggest here. This part of the story is so strong, so tender. I think you've caught the essence of the way daughters feel about their dads, and the way dads will do anything for their daughters. Every time I read this, I think about my own life, and my father, and my own daughter's life too. And each time I read it, I weep — it's that good.

Several times during the editing Hannah Nelson invited Cassandra Day to drop by the office if she was in the area, or just pick up the phone anytime something wasn't clear. Each invitation to visit was politely refused, and the author continued to communicate only by mail.

Hannah also found Cassandra's handwriting hard to read. Cassandra's notes were written with a thin pencil in tiny letters, and the writing had an unusual slant. They looked like that because Zoe was a lefty. After Natalie wrote each note and comment, Zoe copied it out again in her cramped little scrawl. Natalie was sure it was driving her mom nuts, but she didn't want to risk having her handwriting recognized.

Finally, on the fourth pass, the manuscript came back in a new form. The words had all been set into type and laid out in pages. It was called a galley proof, and now each page looked like two side-by-side pages from a book—a real book! Best of all, there were only two Post-it notes on the whole thing, two small errors that were a snap to fix. The book was done.

Two weeks later Ms. Clayton brought Natalie a puffy mailing envelope. It was heavy, and when Natalie pulled the strip to open it, out tumbled two paperback books. Natalie gasped. "The book! It's done!"

But it wasn't the book. It was a paperback printed on flimsy paper, and the cover looked like it had been made from a cheap color Xerox of the jacket. On a black rectangle at the bottom of the cover white letters spelled out this announcement:

Ms. Clayton picked up a handwritten note that had slid onto the table with the books. She glanced at it and then began reading aloud.

Dear Cassandra:
Our marketing department is excited about your book, so we've printed up five hundred of these advance reader's copies. So far, our salespeople have been using our catalog to tell booksellers about your book, and now they will send these ARCs to all their key bookstore accounts. The subsidiary rights department will be sending them to the book clubs, the specialty markets, and our overseas agents. Also, the publicity department will be sending out more than two hundred

ARCs to the trade, institutional, and consumer review media. I'll let you know when we start getting reviews. The hardcover is already in production, and we'll be shipping the advance orders by mid-May. The advance orders aren't great, but a few good reviews should give the sales a boost. I know we rushed a little on the revisions to meet the deadlines, but the book turned out great. You should be very proud.
Yours truly, Hannah.

Natalie held one of the paperbacks with both hands. She *was* proud. It wasn't the real book yet, but it was so close.

Zoe held the other reading copy. She was proud too, but she was also indignant. "What does she mean, the orders aren't so great?

What's the matter with these people? They should be selling these books like crazy. Their publicity people must stink, that's all I can say."

Natalie said, "Remember how my mom said that every year there are more than five thousand new children's books published in the United States? They can't all be bestsellers, Zoe. It's amazing to get one published at all."

Zoe made a face and shrugged. Actually, Zoe had heard only about half of what Natalie had said. Natalie and Ms. Clayton kept talking, but Zoe was busy. She was having a brainstorm. It took only about thirty seconds for the whole idea to take shape, and when it had, Zoe held up the reading copy and said, "Can I have this one, Natalie?"

Natalie smiled and said, "Of course you can." Then Natalie handed her copy to Ms. Clayton and said, "And I want you to have this one. I'll ask my editor to send another one for me."

Ms. Clayton felt choked up, but she swallowed hard and said, "Thank you, Natalie. I'm going to treasure this my whole life."

Absentmindedly Zoe said, "Yeah . . . me too, Natalie." But Zoe's thoughts were elsewhere.

She had just decided it was time for Zee Zee Reisman to develop some new skills. Zoe thought, *I mean, being an agent was fun, but now my client needs something else. What she really needs is . . . publicity!*

CHAPTER 20

Family and Friends

Most books are published quietly. They don't get big ads in the newspaper, they don't get written about in *Time* magazine, and they don't get a publication party. If it's a book by a famous author, or by an author that the publisher wants to impress, then the publisher might send out some invitations and throw a little party. Publishers do this to create some news and, hopefully, sell some books.

So when Zee Zee Reisman called Hannah in mid-April to suggest that Shipley Junior Books might want to throw a little publication party to launch *The Cheater*, Hannah's first reaction was, "It's a nice idea, but I don't think it makes sense."

But then her curiosity took over. All through the negotiations and the editing Cassandra Day and Hannah Nelson had never sat at a worktable together, never gone out to lunch, never even talked on the phone. She felt close to Cassandra Day and had loved their little exchanges about the manuscript. So she thought, *Zee Zee's right. A little party might be nice—and then I'll finally get to meet this lady.*

But Hannah had so much to do that she never focused on the idea. Letha had been piling extra work on her ever since the day she'd been appointed as Cassandra Day's editor.

Then, three days after Zee Zee's call, the first review arrived. It was from *Kirkus Reviews*, and the reviewer gave *The Cheater* special notice with a "star," which is like giving a book an A++. Hannah liked the last three sentences best: "*The Cheater* grabs hold of your heart and never lets go. This writer speaks with a fresh and honest voice, something always welcome in middle-grade fiction. If this first novel is an indication of things to come, then Cassandra Day could emerge as a major new talent."

With the review in her hand Hannah went

upstairs to talk to Tom Morton. Hannah read him the review, and then she proposed a simple publication party on a Friday afternoon in June. Tom Morton agreed instantly, and that was that.

Getting back on the elevator, Hannah had second thoughts. Letha would not be happy about this party, and she'd be furious that Hannah had asked Tom instead of coming to her first.

Hannah almost stepped out of the elevator to go back and call it off. But then she stopped and let the doors glide shut. On the short ride from the sixteenth down to the fourteenth floor, she realized something: Letha was not as scary as she used to be. And then Hannah said to herself, *No, that's not it. Letha is actually scarier than ever. It's just that* I'm *not afraid of her anymore.*

Back in her office Hannah called and left a message for Zee Zee. She said there would be a small "pub party" in honor of Cassandra Day's first novel. It would be on the sixteenth floor of the Shipley Publishing Company building on the second Friday in June. Zee Zee was free to invite anyone she'd like to be there. And everyone was very excited about actually getting to meet the author.

When Zoe got the phone message, she was excited, too. But she kept it to herself.

Natalie had finally gotten Zoe to shut up. For a solid week Zoe had bugged her and begged her and driven her batty. She wanted Natalie to ask her mom if she could bring Zoe and Ms. Clayton to see Shipley Junior Books—just to have a look around.

Natalie thought it wasn't such a good idea, but Zoe wouldn't let up. "It'll be like a field trip for the Publishing Club—and besides, school's almost over. Ms. Clayton probably won't even be our teacher next year."

Finally Natalie agreed to ask her mom if she could bring Zoe and her English teacher to see the publishing office—it wouldn't be a long visit, just in and out.

And her mom said, "Of course you may, sweetie. Just bring them with you after school one day. If I'm too busy to show you around, Ella can do the honors."

So it was all settled. They had an open invitation, and Zoe stopped pestering Natalie. And the day that looked the best for everyone was a Friday afternoon—the second Friday in June.

. . . . .

At three thirty on Friday, June 12, the editorial staff of Shipley Junior Books started straggling up to the sixteenth floor for the publication party. The manuscript had floated around a little, and there was a definite buzz about this book—and early in the day the third starred review had arrived. Everyone was excited about meeting Cassandra Day.

Hannah had already been up to the large conference room twice, once to check on the caterers, and once to be sure that the big banner had been hung up. When Hannah got off the elevator the third time, she could hear that the party had begun. As she walked into the room the first thing she noticed was the camera crew. A woman with a large video camera was taking a shot of the banner while a skinny young man behind her held up a bright light. The young man wore a jacket labeled ABC NEWS. A man with perfect hair, perfect teeth, and a pinstriped suit was talking with Tom Morton. Glancing across the room, Hannah caught the eye of Jody Cross, the publicity director. Jody nodded toward the camera crew, smiled, and gave

Hannah a thumbs-up. Hannah smiled and nodded back. She was impressed that Jody had managed to get some news coverage of such a small event.

When Zoe and Natalie and Ms. Clayton arrived at the fourteenth-floor reception area, Phil buzzed them right in. Her mom wasn't in her office, so Natalie just started walking her guests around the floor. Natalie had been dreading Zoe's little field trip, but now that they'd arrived, she began to enjoy herself.

They started in the art department and slowly worked their way clockwise from area to area. It struck Natalie as odd that there were so few people around, but she just figured that people had left early on a Friday afternoon. It was nice because they didn't have to be as quiet.

Natalie was showing them the stages of a book's cover art, but Zoe interrupted her. "Let's go find your mom, Natalie. You know, so we can ask her some questions too."

Natalie shook her head. "If she's not in her office, it means she's busy. We'll find her later."

Natalie really understood the publishing

process now, and Ms. Clayton had a lot of questions. It was fun to teach her teacher, and it would have been perfect, except that Zoe was so impatient.

They were almost back to her mom's office, and Natalie was standing in Ella's cubicle pointing at the huge pile of envelopes on her worktable. "And that's the slush pile. I've seen it when it was even bigger." Turning around, Natalie said, "And over there in Tim's office—" She stopped midsentence. Letha stood in the corridor outside her office, ten feet away.

Crossing her arms, Letha walked toward them. She smiled faintly and said, "Well, this is a cheery little group . . . and I see you have a tour guide."

Natalie gulped and said, "This is my friend Zoe and my English teacher, Ms. Clayton—and this is my mom's boss, Letha Springfield."

Ms. Clayton stepped around Natalie and held out her hand. "Pleased to meet you, Ms. Springfield."

Letha looked at Ms. Clayton's hand and then shook it briefly. "Yes. Well. We're happy to have you visit us."

Natalie said, "We . . . I was going to wait for my mom, but I don't think she's back yet. If she's not back in a few minutes, then we'll just go. We don't want to bother anyone."

Letha said, "Actually, your mother is . . . just upstairs." Then with an amused smile she added, "But I know she'd want to see you . . . and your friends, too. Just take the elevator up to the sixteenth floor. And be sure to tell her that I sent you to see her."

Natalie nodded and said, "Sure . . . okay. Thanks."

And Letha said, "Oh, you're quite welcome."

As the elevator door opened onto the sixteenth floor an alarm went off in Natalie's head. It didn't sound right. It sounded like . . . like a convention or something. Her first instinct was to push another button—any button—and get away fast. Before she could act, Zoe grabbed her hand and pulled her out of the elevator. Ms. Clayton followed, and Zoe headed right toward the open double doors of a large room where fifty or sixty people were standing around in small groups, talking loud enough to be heard over the talking of everyone else.

Natalie said, "Zoe! I don't think we'd better—"

But Zoe said, "Look, there's your mom," and she tightened her grip on Natalie's hand and headed straight toward Hannah Nelson like a locomotive. Ms. Clayton stopped in the doorway, just barely overcoming her urge to flee.

Halfway across the floor Natalie saw the banner:

THE CHEATER
BY CASSANDRA DAY

CONGRATULATIONS
TO OUR NEWEST AUTHOR!

The camera operator swung to face Zoe and Natalie, and her assistant turned on the lights. All but a few of the people at the edges of the room stopped talking. Everyone craned their necks to see what the camera was targeting. Natalie tried to make sense of the scene around her, but it was happening too fast. In another three seconds Zoe was standing in front of Hannah Nelson.

Hannah had been talking to Tom Morton, trying to act completely at ease. So what if the guest of honor was already thirty minutes late? The lights from the camera suddenly blinded her, and when she looked again, Zoe and Natalie were standing right in front of her.

Zoe looked up into her face and said, "Mrs. Nelson, I know this is going to be a shock, but I want to introduce you to Cassandra Day."

Hannah looked from Zoe to Natalie and then over their heads. Standing in the doorway of the room was a shy-looking young woman wearing a black skirt and a green cardigan sweater. Hannah's face broke into a relieved smile, and she said, "Well, this is . . . great. Come on, Tom, let's go welcome her."

Zoe looked over her shoulder and then turned back and said, "Mrs. Nelson, that's not her." Putting her arm gently around Natalie's waist, Zoe said, "*This* is Cassandra Day. That's her pen name. Cassandra Day is Natalie Nelson."

The camera operator saw it all. As the tape rolled she thought, *It doesn't get better than this*. And she was right.

The camera saw everything so clearly. It saw

the woman look at the girl, completely baffled. It saw the mother's eyes widen, her eyebrows furrow into a question mark and then smooth to understanding. It recorded the ballet of emotions that danced across both faces.

The microphone heard the woman's sharp intake of air, almost a gasp, and then the long breathing out, almost a sigh. And it heard the girl whisper, "It's true, Mom."

Mother and daughter looked at each other for a long moment, and when they hugged, the people and the room and the building and the city around them disappeared.

Pulling away, Natalie looked around and then reached out to take Zoe's hand. "And Mom, this is Zee Zee Reisman." The woman's face did another dance, and then the hug held three.

And standing over in the doorway, tears streaming down her cheeks, Ms. Clayton felt as if she'd just won the New York Marathon.

The publicity director dabbed a tear from her eye and whispered to Tom Morton, "I don't know how Hannah got ABC News to show up, but I'm sure glad she did."

Tom whispered back, "She didn't set this up,

Jody—she said *you* got them here."

The camera was there because Zoe had sent her advance reading copy to a producer at ABC, along with a full explanation of the story behind the book. And she guaranteed the producer that the author would be revealing her identity at a publication party on the sixteenth floor of the Shipley Publishing Company building at four o'clock in the afternoon on the second Friday in June.

The Party was pretty much over by 4:30, and Tom Morton invited all the Shipley employees to get an early start on the weekend. After Zoe and Ms. Clayton said good-bye, Natalie and her mom walked the eight blocks to the Port Authority Bus Terminal.

It was a beautiful June afternoon, but neither of them noticed the blue sky or the springtime bustle along Eighth Avenue. They were too busy. The walk was one long question-and-answer session, punctuated by bursts of laughter, half a dozen hugs, and outrageous impersonations of Zee Zee the agent and Letha the fire-spitting boss.

When their bus rolled down the ramp toward the Lincoln Tunnel, mother and daughter sat side by side, exhausted but glowing.

Hannah cleared her throat. "You know, I almost didn't want you to read this book by Cassandra Day—because of the parts about Angela and her father. I thought those sections might be too hard on you."

Natalie nodded. "Those parts were hard to write. But I wanted to remember Daddy. I wanted to feel what it would be like if he was still here. I don't want to forget about him, not ever."

"Of course not. You won't. He'd be so proud of you right now."

Natalie looked up into her mom's eyes. "Do you think so, Mom?"

Her mom nodded. "I know so."

Two weeks later ABC ran a half-hour story on one of its weekly news shows. The segment was called, "The Publishing Club." The man with the perfect hair and the perfect teeth sat in the studio talking with Zoe, Ms. Clayton, Natalie, and Hannah Nelson. As the story unfolded, the viewers saw location shots of the Deary School, the Linden Room, Shipley Publishing Company, Offices Unlimited, and the law firm of Crouch, Pruitt, and Reisman. At the right places in the story there were short interviews with Arthur Archer, Tom Morton, Robert Reisman, and Fred Nelson. Letha Springfield even got a little air-time, just enough to smile into the camera and say, "I guess it's just the result of experience, sort of a sixth sense I have, but somehow I just *knew* that Hannah Nelson was the right editor for this book."

The program was perfectly timed with the publication of *The Cheater*. It offered the kind of opportunity that a good publicity director dreams about. Jody Cross went right to work, and during the next two weeks Natalie and Zoe spent a lot of time on TV talk shows. They were on *Nickelodeon News for Kids*, plus their picture was on the cover of *People* magazine.

The production manager at Shipley Junior Books almost went crazy trying to keep up with the demand. By the end of August the hardcover book had been reprinted six times, and it was number five on the *New York Times* Children's Bestseller List.

Zoe Reisman received six offers to purchase the rights to use the name of her company, the Sherry Clutch Literary Agency. After consultation with her lawyer, each offer was refused.

Three weeks after the program aired on ABC, the president of one of the largest publishing companies in New York called Letha Springfield. He asked her to become the vice president and editorial director of his Children's Division, and he promised that she would have complete editorial control. His offer was accepted.

By mid-August applications for new student enrollment at the Deary School had reached an all-time high. Arthur Archer and the board of trustees sent a letter of commendation to Ms. Clayton for "embodying so well the ideals of the Deary School." And Mr. Karswell asked her if she'd like to go kayaking some Saturday morning.

The fall alumni newsletter of the Bank Street Graduate School of Education featured an interview with Ms. Laura Clayton. The last question was the hardest for her to answer.

BANK STREET COLLEGE: If you had to give one piece of advice to the men and women who are preparing to become teachers, what would that be?

LAURA CLAYTON: I've been a teacher for only two years now, so I can't pretend to be some great expert. But I think it's important not to be afraid. Don't be afraid to really listen to your students. Remember what it was like to be a kid, and how brave you had to be to try something new. As a teacher, I want to try to be as brave as my students have to be.

One week after the departure of Letha Springfield, Hannah Nelson was promoted. She became the editor in chief of Shipley Junior Books. It was a big jump for her, but Tom Morton felt sure she could handle it.

Sitting in her new office, Hannah Nelson looked out at the Manhattan skyline. She picked up a copy of *The Cheater* off her desk. Opening it, she stared at the title page. She smiled, closed the book, set it back on her desk, and turned to look out the window again.

Then she remembered something. Months ago she had asked Cassandra Day for the last few bits of text needed to complete the book. She recalled handing the note with those final words to her editorial assistant, with instructions to be sure they got added in the right place. Spinning around, she grabbed the book and flipped it open.

There. Just past the title page.

It was the dedication.

Of course, thought Hannah. *How could it be anything else?*

for Dad and Mom,
for Zoe and Ms. Clayton
—N. N.

On the Saturday afternoon before Labor Day the girls sat on the front steps of Zoe's house eating Italian ices, strawberry for Natalie and lemon for Zoe. It was the first time they'd been together in a month.

Natalie and her mom had taken a trip to the Grand Canyon with Uncle Fred. They stayed at the campground in the forest on the North Rim. It was her mom's first two-week vacation in four years. They did a lot of hiking, and a lot of just sitting around, talking, and reading. The peace and quiet was just what Natalie needed.

Zoe and her mom and sisters had spent August at their farm in Connecticut, and Mr. Reisman had driven up on weekends. Zoe loved being at the farm, but the peace was a little too peaceful and the quiet was way too quiet. By the middle of the second week Zoe couldn't wait to get back to the city.

But summer was over now, and school was in the air. Zoe pulled the little wooden spoon out of her mouth and said, "Too bad we don't have Ms. Clayton for English this year."

"Yeah," said Natalie. "And I heard that Mr. Allston is a lot harder, too."

They fell silent again, spooning out chunks of the sweet flavored ice and trying to imagine what seventh grade would be like.

Zoe said, "So, what are you going to do with your first royalty check?"

Natalie shrugged. "College fund, mostly. I might get to spend some, but not much. And there won't be any money coming until next March, you know."

"I know," said Zoe. "I know *exactly* when the royalties get paid, because agents don't get paid until authors do. The checks come every six months. And I know about how much I'm going to get from that first check too. My dad helped me figure it out—it's fifteen percent of whatever they pay you."

Natalie blushed. "I know that's what the contract says . . . but really, Zoe, you should get a lot more than that. I mean, without you that story would just be sitting in a pile at my house."

Zoe wiped a drip off her chin and shook her head. "Maybe so . . . but without your book there'd have been nothing. I helped get it to the right person, but after that, it was all you. My share's just right."

They were quiet, eating again.

Then Zoe said, "You know, when you write another book, Natalie? It won't hurt my feelings if you want to hire a real agent."

Natalie stopped, a last bit of strawberry ice halfway to her mouth. "What, are you crazy? Who could be more real than you?"

The friends looked at each other and smiled.

And Natalie thought, *The way this feels right now? I want to put this feeling into a book someday.*

WHAT'S NEXT FROM THE MASTER OF
THE SCHOOL STORY?

Turn the page for an excerpt from Andrew
Clements's new hardcover novel,

A WEEK IN THE WOODS

0-689-82596-X $16.95
Simon & Schuster Books for Young Readers

Mr. Maxwell looked at the long checklist, and then looked at the calendar, and then he shook his head. It was February fifteenth, and he was sitting at his desk in his classroom at quarter of seven on a Friday morning. And a question formed in his mind: *Why on earth do I do this year after year?* He quickly pushed that thought out of his head and turned back to the checklist.

It had become a tradition at Hardy Elementary School: Bright and early on the

Monday morning of the third week in April, the whole fifth grade piled into three buses and went off for a week in the woods.

And that's what the program was called: A Week in the Woods. It was nature studies and it was environmental science and it was campfires and creative writing and story-telling and woodcraft. It was always the last big event for the fifth graders before they went on to the middle school. It was always fun, always memorable. And the person who always made it happen was Mr. Maxwell, the fifth-grade science teacher.

The kids looked forward to A Week in the Woods. They all loved it. The fifth-grade teachers also looked forward to A Week in the Woods. But not all of them loved it. Not even most of them.

In fact there was a rumor that if Mr. Maxwell ever moved or retired, the program might change. It might become A Day in the Woods. And at this year's early planning meeting, Mrs. Leghorn had been heard muttering, "This is Whitson, New Hampshire, for Pete's sake! *Every* week is a week in the woods!"

Mrs. Leghorn was the fifth-grade math teacher, and if she got her way, the program would become "An Hour in the Woods— Without Me!"

But Mr. Maxwell had originated the program, and this would be his sixteenth year as its director. As always he wanted the fifth graders to have an outdoors experience that they would remember all their lives. So once again it was going to be A Week in the Woods.

Bill Maxwell was a big man. He cut and split his own firewood, and he had the shoulders and arms to prove it. He always wore dress pants and a white shirt and tie to school, and that helped make him look less rugged and a little less imposing. But it was fair to say that Mr. Maxwell had never had a discipline problem in any of his classes. Ever.

At forty-five years old, his thick brown hair was starting to turn gray, but apart from that, he looked like a man ten years younger. He wasn't handsome, but he had a pleasant face, open and honest, with clear blue eyes and a strong jawline.

He had grown up in northern New Hampshire and had majored in environmental studies at the state university. Then at the end of his junior year he took part in an Earth Day event at a grade school. That's when Bill Maxwell discovered that he loved to teach almost as much as he loved the outdoors. He shifted his major into education, and one month after graduation he landed a job in Whitson as a fifth-grade science teacher.

Bill and his college sweetheart had planned to get married, but after she graduated, she took a job as an accountant for a big paper company. The marriage never happened. Young Bill Maxwell could not understand how anyone could work for an industry that did such bad things to the environment.

During his next three years of teaching, Mr. Maxwell lived in a boarding house in the nearby town of Atlinboro. During the summers he painted houses, and he saved every penny. Then he bought forty-five acres of wooded land about fifty miles north of Whitson and built himself a log house. He installed solar panels on the roof, and built a small generator system that made electricity from the stream that tumbled across his property. Before his first winter set in, he figured out how to make a catalytic converter that would reduce the pollution in the smoke from his woodstove.

Mr. Maxwell's younger sister didn't like the idea of him living all alone out in the woods. She worked for the New Hampshire Humane Society, so over the years she had made sure that her big brother always had at least one dog to share his home with.

Mr. Maxwell's mother had more specific ideas. She wanted him to get married and have some children. But whenever she told him that, Mr. Maxwell would smile and say, "Mom, remember? I've *got* children—about a hundred and fifty of 'em every year!"

And five mornings a week, nine months a year, Bill Maxwell drove the quiet country roads from his home to Hardy Elementary School, so he could spend the day with his children. The drive in his old, blue pickup truck took him an hour in each direction, and more in bad in weather, but Mr. Maxwell wouldn't have had it any other way.

Sitting at his desk on the morning of February fifteenth, Mr. Maxwell knew that the program was still eight weeks away. Growing up, Bill Maxwell had been a Boy Scout, then an Explorer Scout, and finally, an Eagle Scout. He took his Scout motto seriously: Be Prepared. Mr. Maxwell's preparations for A Week in the Woods had started back before Thanksgiving.

He had already signed up eighteen parent volunteers to help with the baggage handling, the cooking, and the chaperoning. He'd driven over to the campground at Gray's Notch State Park on a Saturday, and then tramped around in the snow to check out the newest cabins and do a careful bunk count. He'd signed a contract with a Native American man, a Penobscot storyteller who was going to give an evening performance that would include some history about the Abenaki and Pennacook tribes. He had even worked out the menu for each of the thirteen meals and the four evening snacks at the park, and had already placed the order for the food deliveries. Plus he'd taken care of about a dozen other details, not to mention writing and revising and assembling the big information packet. He'd had to have the packet ready to hand out to each fifth grader the day after Christmas vacation, because that had become a tradition too.

True, a lot of the preparations had been completed by February fifteenth, but the checklist went on and on. So Mr. Maxwell scooted his chair up closer to his desk and got to work.

Before the buses arrived, he'd written a letter to the New Hampshire Fish and Wildlife Service, replied to an e-mail from the State Park Ranger Service, and laid out the schedule of events for day three of A Week in the Woods.

As his homeroom kids began streaming through the doorway, Mr. Maxwell made three more neat little marks on his checklist, and then put it away in his file drawer until after school. It had been a productive morning.

That same Friday morning some other preparations were just ending. About two hundred and seventy miles south and west of Whitson, New Hampshire, something was happening.

It was something that was going to have an impact on this year's Week in the Woods, but it wasn't on Mr. Maxwell's long checklist.

There was no way for him to be prepared, not for this. Mr. Maxwell had no idea what kind of trouble was coming his way.

But it was. Trouble was definitely headed north.

GREAT MIDDLE-GRADE FICTION FROM
ANDREW CLEMENTS, MASTER OF
THE SCHOOL STORY

FRINDLE
0-689-80669-8
(hardcover)

0-689-81876-9
(paperback)

THE SCHOOL STORY
0-689-82594-3
(hardcover)

0-689-85186-3
(paperback)

THE LANDRY NEWS
0-689-81817-3
(hardcover)

0-689-82868-3
(paperback)

THE JACKET
0-689-82595-1
(hardcover)

THE JANITOR'S BOY
0-689-81818-1
(hardcover)

0-689-83585-X
(paperback)

A WEEK IN THE WOODS
0-689-82596-X (hardcover)

"Few contemporary writers portray the public school world better than Clements."—*New York Times Book Review*

Aladdin Paperbacks
Simon & Schuster Children's Publishing Division
www.SimonSaysKids.com